Cut Through the Bone

STORIES

Ethel Rohan

"Each piece in Ethel Rohan's Cut Through the Bone is as eerily beautiful as the realistic baby dolls in her story "Lifelike"; and you will find yourself, on multiple occasions, believing that you can hear the stories breathing. In this unforgettable collection, Rohan reveals her mastery in finding the danger of ordinary objects, the way they come alive when her characters hold them in their hands. This is an unsettling and mesmerizing book."

Kevin Wilson,
author of *Tunneling to the Center of the Earth*

"I keep thinking of more and more adjectives in an attempt to describe Ethel Rohan's moving debut collection, which is at turns beautiful and inventive, tender and absurd, quirky and heartbreaking, dark and strange and devastating."

Michael Kimball,
author of *Dear Everybody, How Much of Us There Was,*
and *The Way the Family Got Away*

"Ethel Rohan knows a thing or two about singing with the dragonflies, smashing the mayonnaise jar, and biting Fat Greta. In less than a hundred pages, she offers thirty sharp and shapely stories of Shatter and Scraps, of Mirror and Make Over, of Fee Fi Fo Fum At the Peephole. Like one of her protagonists, I spent a few minutes in the white space, listening for the familiar sound of the car's engine, of the bottles hitting together."

Kyle Minor,
author of *In the Devil's Territory*

Published by Dark Sky Books
Seattle, Washington
All rights reserved.

www.darkskybooks.com

Printed in the United States of America.

ISBN-13: 978-0-615-40093-8
ISBN-10: 0-615-40093-0
First Dark Sky Books Printing, 2010

Book Design: Boo Gilder
Cover Art: Siolo Thompson

For Padraig, Mackenzie, and Teaghan
my always, mo croí

Many of these stories were previously published, sometimes in slightly different forms and with different titles.

Contents

More Than Gone	1
Shatter	5
Mirror	9
Make Over	13
Lifelike	17
On the Loose	21
How to Kill	27
Reduced	29
Gone	33
Endangered	39
Under the Scalpel	43
Scraps	49
All There, Waiting	51
The Bridge They Said Couldn't Be Built	53
Far From Angels	59
The Long Way	63
The Trip	67
Babies on the Shore	75
Found and Lost	77
Vitals	79
The Key	81
Fish	85
Rattle	89
Cracking Open	91
At the Peephole	93
Fee Fi Fo Fum	97
Next to the Gutter	99
The Big Top	101
Crazy	105
Cut Through the Bone	111

More Than Gone

She walks home through the park holding a purple balloon, her arthritic arm protesting. Flowers perfume the air and there's the medicinal smell from the eucalyptus trees. She has come from her youngest granddaughter's fifth birthday party, the balloon a prize of sorts. The party was her first public gathering since Albert's funeral.

She and Albert were married for fifty-six years. He could be lazy and annoying and she was stubborn and pedantic, but they'd come out of the long union the best of friends. She tells all this to the balloon as she walks, not caring about passersby and their indulgent smiles.

She'd enjoyed the festivities, the picnic and magic act especially, but she's tired, drained by the effort of smiling and sustaining chit-chat with so many. Her wool sweater was a mistake, prickling in the heat. She can already feel the rash on her slack, irritated skin. Her granddaughter, more a Goldilocks than a Karen, had beamed while they sang "Happy Birthday." The child presented her with the first slice of cake and she'd felt herself glow pink.

Her children didn't want her to go home alone and had offered to drive. She'd insisted on walking, on enjoying the park. She and Albert had liked to take long walks together and even now she feels him beside her. It comes to her that this impossible presence is what Albert had felt for all those years. He'd lost his right arm in a mortar attack in Korea and to his dying day he could still feel the missing limb, both the pain and the wonder of it. He'd wave the phantom limb and wiggle his invisible fingers, marvel at the empty space. Sometimes, he'd forget himself and offer the phantom limb in a handshake.

For a time after the war, while making love, he'd touch his ghost hand to her body and narrate how he was rubbing her nipples, squeezing and circling her breasts. She hadn't liked that, and had gotten angry. Now, feeling another's touch was such a seldom thing she had to be content with the memory of it. She'd react differently today, she thinks, to Albert's ghost limb. The balloon nods on the breeze.

Home, she kicks off her shoes and ties the balloon to the kitchen table. She pulls off her sweater and drapes it across Albert's armchair, the chair such a comfort, such company, in the room. Her children want her to get rid of it. Never. She'd fall into the space it would leave behind.

She boils water for tea and sets a cup and saucer on the table. With a black marker, she draws two eyes, a nose, and a smile on the balloon. She stands back to admire her handiwork. Throughout the afternoon, she sits with her tea and tells the balloon story after story, about her, and Albert, and their time together.

It's dinnertime, but she's not hungry. Three out of four of her children have phoned to ensure that she made it home okay, that she's doing alright. She's so grateful for her children, she tells the balloon. Its face needs something more, she decides, and again reaches for the black marker.

She adds eyelashes, brows, and hair. The face comes alive and she compliments it on how handsome it looks. The light fades and it's dark outside when she stands and boils more water for tea. Back at the table, the balloon's face is in shadow. She continues with her stories, thinks how the balloon is leaking by the second, emptying. She can just about remember being so young that she'd cry over a burst balloon.

Shatter

The list of accidents grew: a pebble cracked their windshield, a jam jar smashed on the kitchen tiles, a grocery bag burst—shattered glass floating in red wine and egg yolks. Somehow, no one hurt. More, no matter how much she wiped down her kitchen counters and swept her kitchen floor, still she found pieces of glass, glinting up at her. Her husband said she was making something out of nothing.

She worked six twelve-hour shifts a week at the drug-store next to the mall. Supposed to be a starter job out of City College, she'd worked at the store eight years and counting. Wary now—since the accidents—she handled customers' glass purchases with extra care, tense while she scanned and packed the items. The more careful she tried to be, the clumsier she became. During one shift a jar of mayonnaise smashed, during others mustard, beetroot, San Pellegrino. Her manager pulled her aside and asked if she was working under the influence. She blinked and stuttered through his rank breath. Her wits recovered, she told him that if he wanted to get personal, he should know about his halitosis, should clear the green pus from the inner corners of his eyes.

On the bus ride home, a baby in chalk-blue pajamas wailed. His mother bounced him on her knees, rocked him in her arms,

5

shushed and cooed, and waved brightly-colored toys in front of his too red face. Still the baby wailed. She closed her eyes to the baby and his mother, to her reflection in the bus window. They didn't have kids. Something the doctors couldn't explain. Sometimes she thought she only wanted babies because they would give her a break from the drugstore. Other times she thought their childlessness was for the best. On their salaries they couldn't afford a family. Her husband sold life insurance. Seemed people didn't care any more about what they left behind. He insisted on practicing his sales pitches on her. More and more, he sounded like he was pleading with a doctor to save him.

As soon as she arrived home, she phoned her husband at work to remind him they were out of beer and wine.

"Get those sour cream and onion chips, too," she added.

Time was, she purchased the alcohol at a discount from the drugstore. Then her coworkers and manager started to watch and whisper. She chewed harder on the side of her thumb. Maybe she should call her husband back and tell him to forget the chips. Hardly any of her clothes fit any more. Her mouth watered. What was living if she couldn't have her few treats every evening, some chips with wine before dinner after a hard day's work. She thought to phone her mother, but felt too tired. She really should call her sister, too, one of these days. They hadn't spoken in months.

She moved into her living room, turned-on the table lamp with its happy yellow shade, and watched through the window for her husband's silver car to appear. Her reflection stared back, flat and pale. For a mad moment she thought to grab the table lamp and hurl it through the glass. She closed her eyes and steadied her breathing.

A song carried from the radio in the kitchen, something about cheating and revenge. She listened for the familiar sound of the car's engine, of her husband moving up the front path and the bottles hitting together.

Mirror

Daddy gave off that sour Sunday morning smell that I knew meant he wouldn't want to get out of bed until at least the afternoon, but I told him, over and over, that he needed to get up, that it was important. After I whined, tugged on his arm, and repeated "important" enough times he eventually dragged himself from the bed. He pulled on his crumpled trousers and grey shirt, the clothes taken from the floor and stinky with sweat, cigarette smoke, and women's perfume.

I led him down the hall and into his old bedroom, his arm a leash between us. He stood, blinking, bleary-eyed, in the middle of the bedroom he used to share with my mother. He grumbled, unimpressed with my idea of important.

"Please," I said.

He held his head with both hands, said he was inside a dark cage. I ran to the windows and pulled back the sheer curtains, let as much light as possible into the room. He stared at the bed, his old bed, and at the hardwood floor, his old floor. I'd pulled out Mother's dresses from the wardrobe and laid them out on the pillows and patchwork quilt, and lined-up her old purses, scarves, and shoes on the floor.

For months, I'd secreted myself away in my parents' old bedroom and dressed-up in all my mother's old things, primped and pranced in front of the wardrobe's full-length mirror. Inside the mirror, my mother smiled back at me, fussed over my hair and the zip of my dress. She always cooed at how lovely I looked. I told her I wasn't nearly as beautiful as she was. I didn't tell her that I wanted to fold her up into a tiny, perfect square and stitch her to the skin over my heart.

One early morning, when I was five, my mother disappeared. She walked out our front door and was never seen or heard from again. I believed she'd return one day soon, always soon, but Daddy didn't like me to ever talk about that. She was gone, he said, and we needed to get on with things. I never asked what things, but I fretted. Whenever I worried Daddy might marry again, I reminded myself that the priest or the government would never allow it. Daddy couldn't ever remarry. Mother was alive, and until she returned we were stuck in limbo, purgatory on earth. I supposed Daddy could get in another woman and have babies with her, like Mr. Mooney from two streets over had done, making his family the talk of the neighborhood. Only I didn't think Daddy could bear to give people any more material for gossip. I knew I couldn't.

Over the years, kids in school had let slip their parents' lies, while others even delighted in telling me: My mother had drowned herself in the river, or run off with another man, or my father had killed her and buried her in our back garden, right underneath the red rose bushes he'd planted on the very day she went missing. I didn't believe any of those terrible stories. My mother would never leave Daddy, never leave me. And Daddy most certainly hadn't harmed her. He hated to kill even a mouse. Someone had taken her away, a bad man. Or she'd fallen into the river and drowned. But she would never have gone willingly, never have made that awful choice.

The red rose bushes scared me. I didn't like to go anywhere near them. Yet I felt drawn to them again and again. I sometimes pushed myself as close to the flowers as I dared, and leaned forward, as far as I could, and stretched out from my waist, my nose inching closer and closer. The moment I sniffed the rose's dark petals I whirled around and sprinted up the garden to the house, the grass slippery and grabbing, running, running as if from something deadly. As much as I didn't want to hear it, my nose wouldn't shut up: The flowers smelled just like my mother.

Daddy wouldn't get into one of my mother's dresses. I held up her moss-green dress with the tiny yellow buttercups, my favorite, and pleaded. Daddy shook his head, a savage look on his face. I climbed into the dress, and wrapped my mother's brilliant orange silk shawl around my shoulders, slipped around inside her strappy brown platforms. In the mirror, my mother's hand covered her mouth and eyes filled with pride. My belly fluttered, and I went falling, falling through a peach cloud. I turned to Daddy. His face changed to the color of concrete. He grabbed my head, his fingers in my skull and thumbs in my cheekbones. I made hurt sounds and tried to get out of myself. Daddy bared his teeth, his face now filled with the horror of someone suffocating, and said "God, God" while he shook me.

I slapped at his arms, his chest. He jumped away from me. We stared at each other, stunned, breathless. I felt I had holes in my head and face from the crush of his fingers. He dropped to his knees and cradled me tightly in his lap, hid his face in my shoulder. Inside the glass, my mother flailed, a tree in a storm, trying to get to us.

Make Over

She was riding the bus, imagining herself in a boat on a colorful lake, singing with the dragonflies, when she first felt the woman try to get out of her chest. She jerked upright, her hand at her sternum, and scanned her fellow passengers, sure they could see the commotion inside. No one paid her the slightest attention. The woman inside her chest gritted her teeth and pushed against breastbone, determined to break out.

At home, she drank three glasses of red wine and stupefied the woman.

Days later, she remembered the long, blond wig she'd bought weeks back for her daughter, for the school play. Alone in the house, she placed the wig on her dark head and studied herself in the mirror, another person entirely. She smiled.

She took to wearing bright red lipstick, large hanging earrings, and tight-fitting clothes. She painted her nails the colors of the rainbow. The woman inside her chest jumped and clapped. She worked at the music store part-time, around her daughter's schedule. Her boss also applauded her new image. The regulars grinned and whooped.

Soon, she stopped removing the wig and racy clothes before her husband and daughter returned home in the evenings. Her husband complained they were the talk of the neighborhood, of their daughter's school.

She mussed his hair. "Fame at last."

He grabbed her wrist, tight.

Her daughter cried, said she couldn't bring her friends around anymore.

She said, "Then they're not your real friends."

When she bought the hot-pink plastic karaoke machine and spent almost all her time in front of the TV screen belting out songs, the microphone her umbilical cord, her husband pressed her to see a professional. Her daughter cried and raged. She sang over their histrionics, her mind made up. She had to let her music out.

She circled the classifieds in red pen and hoped to pick-up an evening gig or two.

"Grow up," her husband said.

While she sang, the woman in her chest danced, spun and spun. She urged her husband and daughter to sing with her, to dance along. They refused, and condemned her looks, her singing, her lies.

She had never felt more honest.

One morning in bed, her husband said he couldn't look at her anymore, that her madness kept him awake at night.

His eyes wet, he said, "Remember when we were happy?"

But here she was, happy now. He tried to remove her wig and her microphone from under her pillow. She slapped at him.

Her daughter rushed into the room. "Please stop, Mommy, stop."

She looked at her daughter and saw a bleeding wound, heard the gurgle of too much to bear. The woman inside her chest kicked and swung her arms, huffed like their faulty ceiling fan.

She lifted the wig off her head, rubbed off her lipstick with her forearm, and handed over her microphone.

Her daughter fell into her arms. "You're back, Mommy, you're back."

Inside her chest, the woman shrieked, clawed.

Lifelike

When UPS delivered the first lifelike baby doll, Sandy clapped and shrieked. The newborn replica, dressed in a powder-blue onesie, came fitted with a heartbeat, glossed nails, ginger human hair, and mottled, veined skin. The doll so realistic Rob drew back, his scalp crawling.

"Isn't he darling?" Sandy asked.

Rob refused to touch the doll or to help choose its name. Sandy sat up most of the night with the doll, and decided on "Pearce."

After breakfast, she phoned her employer and cited "a family matter," asked for a week's leave. Rob swallowed hard on his bagel.

She rang off, and met his cold stare. "What?"

Over the next several weeks, she crammed the guest bedroom with these lifelike dolls and their white wicker bassinets. Rob's rants and ultimatums went ignored. The evening she announced she had quit her job to stay home full-time with the babies, Rob fell dumbstruck. She lifted up one of the pink adorned dolls and cooed.

Rob suggested they go out to dinner. She needed to get away from the house, he pressed, and those dolls. She refused.

A movie, he tried again. She loved movies. They could watch something at home, she countered. They weren't a couple any more, he argued, the dolls everything to her now. She'd stopped seeing her friends. The phone hardly rang. They argued on and on, but she wouldn't leave the house, not without her babies.

At the paper company, he worked late into the evenings. They needed the extra income now that she was unemployed and splurging on more dolls and their accessories. So many dolls that they'd overflowed into the second guest bedroom. She hadn't noticed that the tropical fish had died.

He asked her again to go out. She refused again, and cradled the yellow clad doll. He stormed out to Malarky's, a local he'd started to frequent. He sipped ice-cold beers and listened to country music on the juke box, gabbed with the half-deaf bartender.

He closed the bar, and returned home to find Dollsville in darkness, save for the jaundiced glow through the far bedroom window courtesy of "The Cow Jumped over the Moon" themed lamp. He trudged inside, and paused outside the yellowed bedroom, its door ajar. Sandy sang soft and low, *Daddy's going to buy you a mocking bird.*

She sat on the rocking chair with her back to him, only the doll's bald head visible in the crook of her arm. He moved deeper into the room and watched, disbelieving. Sandy's bloodied finger moved in a circular motion over the doll's naked chest, smearing it red. He made some exclamation.

Sandy moved out of the chair, the doll clutched to her breasts. She backed away from him, blood trickling down her hand. He spotted the kitchen paring knife under her chair, realized she'd nicked herself.

He said, "Tell me you know they're not real?"

She shook her head, glared.

He reached for the doll. "You better see to that finger."

Her eyes filled. "She won't settle."

He paused, then, "Let me try." He eased the doll away from her, and resisted the urge to throw it across the room.

"Maybe she could sleep with us tonight?" she asked.

He looked into his wife's pale, startled face and saw the mix of fear and hope. He nodded. Her smile almost made his legs buckle.

Throughout the night, he jerked awake, imagining he could hear crying. He checked first on his wife and then on the doll between them.

On the Loose

The burly guy in the gray hoodie walked into the gas station just before midnight and set Tracy's heart racing. He barreled toward her, dark stains on the front of his sweatshirt and his white-washed jeans belted around fat thighs. A lit cigarette hung from his meaty mouth, right next to his silver lip piercing. She felt a flicker of recognition, then cold fear.

Tracy asked him to kill the cigarette, her voice humiliatingly meek. He ignored her and moved through the aisles, muttering, his arms flailing. She warned him he would set off the smoke alarm, if not one of the gas pumps.

He whirled around. "Don't you tell me what to do, girl."

The way he said "girl" she felt slapped. He'd been in before, a week back, him and that other scumbag who'd spit chewing gum in her face. They'd run out right after, laughing. She gripped the edge of the counter and tried to stop trembling. A sly glance at the security cameras confirmed they were on.

In the three months she'd worked at the station, she had already hit the alarm five times. After the last incident, the whole "I swear it looked like a gun in his pants" fiasco, her boss told her that unless someone had a knife to her throat, he didn't want her to hit any "motherfucking alarm" and mess-up his insurance or piss off the local cops. "Nobody likes paperwork, you hear?"

While her boss's warning echoed in her head, the guy grabbed a six-pack of beer from the fridge and managed to knock over some cans. The cans crashed to the floor, thud, thud, thud, and rolled back and forth. He called her over. She stood rooted to the spot. He shouted. She struggled to the fridge, felt as if her ankles were chained together.

He pointed at the beers on the dull, once green tiles. "Pick them up."

She held his fiery gaze. "That's not my mess."

He raised his fist. She drew back.

"Get," he said between bared teeth.

She bent to the cans, steeling herself against the blow to the back of her head that she felt sure was coming.

"That's it, that's the girl."

She straightened, and held the cans to her like babies, encouraged by his praise.

He ordered her to put the cans back in the fridge, and moved behind her. She obliged, her insides turning to sludge.

He shuffled to the counter and placed the six-pack of beer on top of the stack of newspapers. She returned behind the counter, glad of the barrier between them. Her eyes scanned out front. She prayed the driver at Pump One would notice something amiss and come inside or call the police.

Her hand reached for the cash register. She told herself it would be over soon. He would leave or help would come, and she'd have something to tell her roommates tomorrow.

"Not so fast," he said.

Her fingers froze on the register's cool plastic buttons.

"I'm not finished yet." He dropped his cigarette butt.

The car at Pump One pulled away, making her want to cry. She tried to work some saliva back into her mouth, and managed to croak, "What else?"

He reached inside his back pocket and pulled out a rolled joint.

Tracy forced a smile. "You can't do that here."

"Can't I?"

She tried to sound conspiratorial. "I think you'd better go. The cops always patrol here."

He dragged on his joint, and gestured it toward her. She shook her head.

His smile had an edge like a cliff. "You are a good girl, aren't you? A real good girl."

She pinned her smile to her face. *Just humor him*, she thought. *He'll leave, and I'll look for another job first thing.*

He slapped the counter, making her jump. "You going to join me or what?"

"I can't, I have real bad asthma." Her mother hadn't wanted her to move out here, had warned that San Francisco's fog wouldn't be good for her. She hadn't wanted her to work the gas station either, said something just like this would happen.

He laughed, making a "whee" sound. "You got one of those inhaler things?"

She nodded.

His face hardened, his eyes like something dead. "Let me see."

She reached inside her purse, and rummaged for her inhaler, all the while trying to hide her wallet. He grabbed the inhaler, and pushed its tip inside his mouth. She felt like he'd put her in there.

He pumped the inhaler, twice, three times, four.

"I don't think you should—"

He pulled the inhaler from his lips, silver strings of saliva strung to it like the threads of a cobweb. He danced about in a circle, shouting about how his chest felt open, huge, how nothing so easy had ever set him going like this.

He ripped open the cardboard beer container and offered her one. Tears of condensation slid down the bottle. She knew not to refuse. They twisted off the beer caps and dropped them to the floor. The caps made a tinkling, sad sound. He chugged his beer, and talked, double-fast. She watched his meaty lips separate and come together, the glint of his piercing, and caught clips of his rant about people she didn't know.

He grabbed her shirt and pulled her to him. She cried out, a sound like her roommate's cat made when he was hurt. She willed somebody to come into the store, anybody.

He made to kiss her, but then pushed her away. "You got a mustache."

Her hand shot to her upper lip.

His eyes raked the shelves above them, grabbed a packet of razors.

She jumped for the alarm, fuck paperwork, but he caught her arm and twisted it up and behind her back. He marched her to the restroom, and pushed her inside.

"Don't, please—"

He threw the packet of razors, hit her full in the face. "Shave that mess off."

She covered her face with the crook of her arm. "Please—"

He shouted again.

Her hands shaking, she freed the razor from its packaging, and splashed water on her face. The soap slipped out of her hands, and she had to chase it around the filthy sink.

"Get on with it, girl."

"My name's Tracy."

"I don't give a fuck."

Something spread inside her like a black spill, a sense that this was the confrontation she'd worked toward her whole life, this the one show-down she wasn't going to walk away from, or bow her head to, or smile and swallow down everything she wanted to say and do.

"My name's Tracy."

He pushed his face close to hers. "Excuse me?" His breath stung her nostrils.

"Call me Tracy."

He grabbed the razor and touched it to her face. "I know what I'll trace."

She closed her eyes, and made horrible noises.

He threw the razor in the sink, the sound of something breaking. "Now shave."

She soaped and shaved her upper lip, avoiding the mirror as much as possible. The fluorescent ceiling light warmed her head. On the last stroke, she nicked herself.

"Stupid girl." He hooked his hand under her chin and pulled her toward him. He stuck out his thick red tongue, its back caked in dirty white, and licked across her mouth and up under her nose. Then he kissed her hard, his piercing bruising her mouth. She tasted salt from his sweat, from her blood.

He pulled back his lips, showing more of his brown teeth and pale gums, his eyes crazy-wide. "I'm gonna eat you."

He pushed her against the wall. She hit the back of her head, heard the whack, but didn't feel anything. He moved toward her. She gritted her teeth and lurched forward, kneed his groin hard and rammed her three middle fingers into his left eye. He spun about, his hands at his face. He roared.

She raced past him, out of the restroom, out of the store, and into the dark street. Someone shouted, not him. He was still inside. She ran, coughing, struggling to breathe. Her chest tightened. Wheezing, sweating, she pictured her lungs flapping like the wings of a frightened bird, her airways shrinking, shutting down. Even as her legs gave way and she sank to the sidewalk, she felt the thrum of triumph. She'd gotten away. It would feel so good to tell her mama, to make her proud. A woman kneeled next to her and gripped her hand, stroked her hair. A man tucked his rolled jacket under her head. Sirens wailed, louder and louder. All she needed to do now was to breathe, breathe big.

How to Kill

Ann fried the eggs, careful not to break the yolks. Her thoughts remained on the fake gypsy woman from the bar the previous night, her and her stupid tarot cards. Fred appeared at her feet and thumped his tail, whimpered. She tossed him a sausage. He barked and snatched the meat mid-air.

Matt appeared in the kitchen, disheveled. He reeked of stale beer. She poured coffee. He scratched his hairy stomach, his shirt riding up and down. She put the food in front of him, and turned back to the oven. He couldn't face a fry, he complained.

"Your choice," she said.

The supposed gypsy had long, greasy hair. Gold hoop earrings peeked from the dirty strands. Her gold arm bangles jingled while she dealt and lifted the cards. A mushroom smell off her breath and earthy whiff off her skin. She accepted payment in Tequila Sunrises choked with cherries.

At first, Ann had waved off the tarot cards for nonsense, but the woman's gravelly voice and dark, probing eyes held her mesmerized. When she claimed she could see a baby where there was no longer a baby, Ann felt snakes wrap around her body and cinch her chest.

...

Matt speared a sausage, and gestured at her coffee mug, questioning.

"I can't eat breakfast, not since ...." her voice trailed off.

He wiped his mouth with the back of his hand, stained himself with ketchup.

She continued, "Not since the morning sickness."

He called Fred over, fed him bacon.

She remembered the drugstore with its endless aisles and harsh yellow lights. He had waited outside in the parking lot. When the test proved positive, he had looked straight at her for the first time since she'd told him maybe, his face red with anger, blame, disbelief.

She pushed away her coffee mug. His eyes followed hers to the wall calendar and away again, a sullen expression on his face. He had acted so sweet on the day of the clinic, opened doors, stroked her hair, and reassured her over and over.

After, he had helped her into their bed with its clean sheets and hot water bottle, and held her until she fell asleep. She could still smell his relief.

He pushed away his breakfast plate. The leftovers looked violated.

He moved to the radio on the Formica counter and turned-up the volume too loud. The Smiths.

She gripped the sides of her chair and spoke over the noise. "What would have been so terrible about us having the baby?"

He walked out of the kitchen, and the apartment.

She cupped her coffee mug and held onto its warmth. Fred padded over, looked to the door, and whined. She patted his bony head.

Reduced

A father from our daughter's kindergarten class sent invitations to his art exhibit downtown. The white card was premium stock and edged in gold. The envelope was lined with rainbow-colored silk paper and felt smooth beneath my fingers. My wedding was the only occasion I had ever sent such fancy invites. The kind of invite you had a drink with.

We arrived at the gallery. Its walls were white-washed behind the oil paintings, and the lights hung low from the white ceiling, stalactites. Waiters dressed in black-and-white and with dark slicked-back hair moved through the crowd. They offered white and red wine in stemless glasses. I reached for the red. My husband shot me a look and requested water. We made small talk with the other parents, about the weather, economy, and rumors that the school principal would take early retirement.

As soon as I could get away, I visited with each of the twenty-six paintings. I pictured what I would change: Put the red dog between the trout's jaws; the church spire atop a prison; make a forest of the men, women, and children, and float the massacred trees in a field of bright green blood. My imagination flowed along with the wine. Not that I was an artist. I liked to reimagine things.

...

We strolled arm-in-arm from the gallery to a nearby restaurant, the air cold and moon full. The restaurant smelled of garlic and basil. My husband gestured at my wine-colored lips. I pictured the bloody hues there, trapped in the crevices. I chewed at the stains. My teeth were also discolored, he added. It always happened. I forced a toothless smile and told him about my afternoon with Mia, our trip to the zoo. One lemur had mirrored Mia's hand gestures and waved, pointed, and clapped.

He sniffed. "Monkey see, monkey do."

The waiter, soft cinnamon eyes and black hair shiny as plumage, removed my wine glass. I ordered another.

"Your fifth? Sixth?" my husband asked.

I looked out the window. A girl pulled an aggressive three-point turn in her red SUV and snagged the parking space right outside the restaurant. I should drive like that, take.

My husband used his dinner napkin to wipe the back of his neck and his forehead. He rubbed the napkin repeatedly over his hair, ten, twelve strokes. I wanted to snatch the napkin and throw it at him. Animals in the zoo primped themselves in front of everyone. His doing that, it reduced us. Sweat broke again on his forehead. I pictured both of us melting right there at the table, watched as we struggled and mouthed, tried to reach for each other, but we were powerless, voiceless. Then, then we shrank, slowly, slowly, and dissipated to puddles on our chairs, his clear and mine red.

From the ceiling, clusters of silver balls, the same type used for Christmas decoration, hung low from thin steel cords. I asked my husband if they weren't like arms reaching down from the moon with miniature orbs at their ends, the moon offering us parts of her.

His face darkened. "You're drunk."

I lifted my wine glass. "I'm imaginative."

30

I tried to relax back into how loose and soft I felt, my senses blunted and edges padded. Where nothing hurt. But the floating feeling was gone.

He rubbed his eyes with his fingers, weary, sad. "You promised."

I swallowed and looked into my wine glass, pictured my parents inside. They sat facing each other with their knees pulled to their chests and heads tipped back, their mouths open, filling. I drained my glass and waved to the waiter.

Gone

My fingers traced the diagonal scars that ran from my armpits and across the memory of my breasts, the stitches long dissolved and the red, angry skin faded to pink. My other hand moved to my stomach and traveled up and down its long vertical scar, this one more purplish than pink. The scars dry and flaky. Fish spines.

I listened to the birdsong outside my bedroom window and decided to put off going to the hospital until the afternoon. I was no longer a patient, but sometimes returned to volunteer. I liked to hold the babies that didn't have visitors, to breathe in their freshness and sing them to smiles. I had my first Friday off in months from the diner and felt glad to be free of the customers' small-talk, of their complaints and ogles. One thing I was never free of was the diner's deep-fried air. It hung all around me and wouldn't wash away. Still, I liked my job well enough and could do it robot-like while I day-dreamed.

Jason, a handsome, square-jawed, blue-eyed regular who wasn't coy about his wish to have me on the menu, would be disappointed by my absence. I smiled into my pillow. Sometimes, while I carried the trays and wiped down the tables, I fantasized about Jason and me going out together, to a movie or a nice restaurant.

I wouldn't let myself think beyond that. I couldn't imagine the two of us alone together.

My neighbor's colicky baby wailed. Their back door smacked closed. I moved from my warm bed to the window. My neighbor stood in her dark pajamas and bare feet in the grass, her hands on her hips and dark head turned up to the sky. I tried to remember her name. The baby's cries climbed and my neighbor's hands covered her ears. Months back, her husband had deployed to Iraq. He had yet to meet his son. She was always polite, but distant, and seemed to want to keep to herself. That suited me. In addition to the fussy newborn, she had two little girls. Her name came to me, Nancy. I dressed quickly, tried not to look at my too-big bed.

Just as I reached my front door, the kitchen phone shrilled. It was likely my dad, and if I didn't answer, he'd worry. It turned out to be Jason. His voice sent me bobbing in warm, shiny water. He had bribed the new busboy for my number, said he never again wanted to have breakfast without me. He'd never had breakfast with me, I corrected, just delivered by me. The sneaky, small-eyed busboy had also given him my address. Jason asked to come over. I warned him not to dare. He chuckled. I pictured his thick, shiny-with-maple-syrup lips and again felt a rush of pleasure.

"I want to show you my latest drawing," he said.

The next door baby continued to cry. "I have to go, seriously."

"I drew you."

My insides recoiled, and I rushed the receiver down.

Jason sometimes brought his sketches to the diner, mostly of hawks, trees, the ocean, and everyday people. Gifted, he managed to bring out in his subjects something I'd never have noticed: the hawks' intelligent eyes and the blue in their black talons; green leaves so smooth, shiny, and thick I wanted to pet them; and emotions in people's faces that lifted right off the page. He was gifted, yes, but he'd no right to draw me without my permission, to take from me like that.

I walked along the side of Nancy's house and called out over her wooden fence. The baby wailed. Moments later, Nancy pulled open her front door. She stood tall and thin and appeared ill. Her face was pale, and she had greenish circles under her eyes. Her long gray-black hair was messed and unwashed. I tried not to react to her body odor, and followed the baby's cries upstairs. The unclean smell pervaded the house and yet everything, the carpet, wallpaper, and furnishings, looked washed-out. There was also the smell of burnt toast.

The baby lay on his side in his crib, his face a dangerous red. His eyes were scrunched shut and his mouth was open wide. His colorless fingers gripped the bars on his crib, and I had to peel the spongy digits free. I lifted him, and he roared. I hugged him to my shoulder and shushed at his damp ear. Nancy apologized, explained. She had tried everything. I urged her to take a shower and to nap. I would stay. Nancy protested. She couldn't, she shouldn't. I insisted. His mother gone, the baby kicked his legs inside his yellow pajamas and jerked his fists. He cried harder. His large bald head pushed and rooted at my prosthetic bra and his greedy grunts turned frantic. I had only my baby finger to offer. The force of his suck hurt and frightened me, could rip my finger right off.

I carried him outside to the garden, the sky boy-blue and the sun hidden behind clouds. The cool breeze startled him into silence. I bounced him in my arms and praised and cooed. He started-up again. I sang to him, soft and low. Overhead, the plovers circled and seemed to listen, to sing back. The baby quieted and closed his eyes. We returned inside. I cradled him in his rocking chair and breathed-in his sweet-and-sour milky smell. My thoughts returned to Jason. I wondered how he'd drawn me.

For sure, at thirty-two, he would never have depicted me as scarred, breastless, and barren. I had chosen to hedge my bets and allowed the surgeons to get ahead of the white spots in my breasts and lymph nodes, to cut away at me.

On the street, a car slowed and stopped. Its door closed. I held the baby and my breath and strained to hear.

Jason waited on my front porch for over an hour. Twice, I'd signaled from the baby's window and indicated he should go. He waved away my gestures and leaned back against my front door, his black artist's case by his hip. I left Nancy recharged and her baby still asleep. At the end of her front path, I almost turned left instead of right, but pressed on to my house and Jason. His easy smile almost made me bolt. He wore faded, ripped jeans and a tight red t-shirt. Red, despite everything, was still my favorite color. We sat on the barstools at my messy kitchen island, there junk mail and other bits of me scattered about. I wished everything was more in order.

I followed his gaze to the reproduction Frida Kahlo on the opposite wall. He scrutinized Kahlo's naked breasts, open torso, shattered spine, body harness, and the nails that punctured her flesh. He turned back to me with an uncertain smile. I offered coffee, but he refused. His attention turned to the single pine chair at my tiny kitchen table. I'd put its mate in the garage. He reached for his artist's case. I jumped at the coffeemaker.

I put a mug of steaming coffee in front of him, and told him about the baby next door, the babies in the hospital. In the end, I was the one who reached for his portfolio. He'd captured me in profile, as I scribbled a customer's order, the obligatory smile on my face. My dark hair was tied up and its loose strands caught behind my ear, curling toward my throat. My prosthetic breasts pushed against my pink uniform, smaller than my real breasts. He'd shaded my face, trapped me in shadow.

I pushed the drawing aside. "It's not me."

He looked from me to the drawing and back again, perplexed.

I reappeared in the kitchen, my shirt and bra removed and the black camisole clinging to my small boy chest. I dropped my hands to my sides. He searched my face, swallowing. I told him how much was gone. He held my gaze.

"You want to try again?" I asked, my face hot.

He nodded. I tried to slow my breath, to stop shaking. He moved the pine chair to the window. Seated, the sun warmed my head and shoulder. I peeled off the camisole and dropped it to the floor. I looked straight at him. His pencil danced over the paper.

Endangered

I landed an office manager position on Wall Street and moved into a studio in Greenwich Village. Jubilant, I invited my younger sister up for the weekend.

"Want to rub my nose in it, huh?" Sally said.

That first night, she wanted to watch lions kill antelope and mount each other on Animal Planet. We drank red wine out of plastic cups and buttered popcorn out of cereal bowls. The salt stung my lips. Live music carried through the window from Jack's, "Walking on Sunshine." Sally had forgotten her fake ID. I was twenty-two and had five years on her. We finished one box of wine and opened another.

The next morning, Sally complained that the noise of the coffee grinder had woken her. She played with her blueberry pancakes, and glared into her percolated coffee, asked if I had instant.

I proposed our itinerary, the usual suspects.

She said, "I heard The Museum of Sex rocks."

We said little on the subway to the Museum. The excursion was Sally's attempt to outrage me. I offered her cinnamon chewing gum. She looked at me like I was shit on her shoe, said she hated cinnamon. I rolled foil wrapping and flicked it at her head.

...

Inside the Museum, Sally headed straight for the "Naked Ambition" exhibit, a large dimmed room wall-to-wall with oversized porn prints. She stared, open-mouthed, and touched where it said "no touching." I wanted to slap down her hands. Oblivious, she wore a happy, slobbery dog face. I wondered if we'd ever felt close. I seemed to remember yes, way, way back.

"The Sex Life of Animals" exhibit rendered in graphic, unapologetic detail just how animal urges weren't any different than our own. "The Sex Life of Robots" was a porn movie starring remarkably flexible machines. I refused to enter the "Techniques Exhibit." Sally plowed ahead.

She exited, beaming, looked like she'd wet her underwear. "I'm famished."

In the diner, I said, "That was bordering on sick."

Her color rose. "How could you not get how tight that was?"

"'Tight?'"

She dropped her sandwich onto her plate, its insides spilling out, and tossed a tomato slice, hit my cheek.

I wiped my face with my napkin.

"Can't you ever stop being so fucking together?" She threw her pickle, caught me in the eye and made it stream.

Before I'd time to recover, she threw her wad of turkey slices at my chest. I winced. She licked her fingers and smirked.

I grabbed the turkey and threw it back, struck her right between the eyes.

She fired her side salad, got me full in the face.

I returned the soggy lettuce with force, splattered her front.

By the time the Manager appeared, Sally's potato salad had slid down my chest and onto my lap.

Outside the diner, I went east and Sally west.

On the subway home, I felt so stupid in my stained clothes, and worried they'd start to sour and smell. From the empty seat beside me, I swear I heard Sally laugh. Only she sounded more scared than amused. We entered the dark of the tunnel. The Museum's video of the pandas' coupling came back to me, how frantic and strained they had seemed, as if they knew they were in danger of extinction, knew they wouldn't make it.

Under the Scalpel

At O'Hare Airport, Mom entered the arrivals lounge dressed in a black turtleneck sweater, a large straw hat, and dark, oversized sunglasses, but there was no hiding her botched facelift. Its results just as awful as she'd claimed. Her colorless lips were stretched straight and her face pulled back so tight, the bones looked ready to burst through. Purple-red bumps and puckers, like a shoddy hemline, shouted from her jaw.

We hugged, both of us crying. She smelled like wilted flowers. People milled about us. Several stared.

While we waited on her bags, John phoned.

I stepped away. "It's awful," I whispered. "Worse than you can imagine."

Mom turned her head, frantic and owl-like, searching for me. I snapped my phone shut.

When we arrived home, John spluttered and turned bright red.

Dinner dragged. Mom had removed her hat, but still wore her sunglasses and turtleneck. I regretted the candles, their eerie flicker making her look grotesque. Her shaky hand returned to her graying hair. She fussed and patted. She couldn't bring herself to go to the hair salon, she repeated, to venture outside for anything. Except to get to me, she finished. I couldn't hold her watery gaze. She gave John her "you're dismissed" look.

Once he left, Mom drew a deep breath and removed her sunglasses. "I'm hideous, aren't I?"

It took all my strength not to register my horror. The skin around her eyes was pulled so fast to her hairline, her eyeballs looked unattached, floated in blood.

I swallowed. "It's going to get better. The bruises will go and the scars will fade and—"

"Don't lie. I'm disfigured, not delusional."

I squeezed her hand and struggled not to cry. "We'll get the surgery fixed. We will."

She covered her face with her napkin. I rushed around the table to her.

Later, in bed, I explained, again, to John that several experts had warned Mom to wait at least a year before considering corrective surgery.

"So much for getting back at your dad," he said.

"The surgery wasn't just about him." How could Mom compete with Dad's reinvention? He'd announced he was gay, in love, and up and left her.

John lifted his head, his hair up at the back. "You know you can't fix this, right?"

"Don't say that. I don't want to hear that."

I turned my back to him. He sighed hard enough to stir my hair.

The next day, Sunday, arrived warm and sunny. I suggested we take a drive someplace. Mom panicked, and hyperventilated into a paper bag. She still hadn't recovered from the stares on the plane and in the airports, said that I had to realize she hadn't left her apartment since the operation and had her groceries, everything, delivered. She went in search of her Valium.

"I think she needs professional help," John said.

"I told you, she has to wait at least a year—"

"I mean psychological help."

"You're not helping," I said. "You're really not."

I went online, and researched what could be done. One website for burn victims suggested wigs and specialty make-up. Over the phone, I purchased a medium length wig with lots of volume and, from another store, several items of corrective make-up. All promised to help hide and heal the scars. I arranged to have the purchases couriered over. John would flip at the expense, but I didn't care. That evening, Mom appeared to dinner in her new wig and make-up. They didn't help nearly as much as I'd hoped. She looked sad and garish, a factory doll thrown to the reject pile.

The following morning, John went to the office as usual. Mom suffered another panic attack when she learned that I also intended to go to work.

"I can't stay on my own," she said. "I don't trust myself."

My stomach tightened. I offered her platitudes and chamomile tea. She gulped another Valium, and paced the rug in tight circles.

"Wouldn't your father love to see me now?" she said. "Him and his dandy man."

"You know that's not true," I said.

She returned to the armchair. "I could kill that surgeon."

"Stop, Mom," I said.

"You have no idea. I can see it all in my head. I wait for him in the hospital parking lot and right as he's about to get into his fancy car I run at him, my gun aimed. I tell him how lucky he is, about to die instantly when I've had to live like this. I squeeze the trigger, and blow a hole clear through his face. Then I put the barrel of the gun under my chin—"

"That's enough," I said. "Please." I held her.

She fell against me, her hands over her face. "I feel like everything's conspiring against me."

"Please, Mom, don't."

"I can't go on like this. I can't."

I felt faint with fright, the top of my head lifting off. It was like watching her come up for one last breath before she drowned.

I steadied myself. "We're going to fix your face, we will. And meanwhile you can stay here as long as you like. You can move-in permanently if you want?"

She sat up straight on the chair and searched my face, her eyes wet. Her lips pecked the backs of my hands and my face. "What would I ever do without you?"

Her words, like her kisses, pierced me.

Before everything happened with Mom, I had promised to host a dinner at the house for my best friend Carrie's thirtieth birthday. John didn't see why we couldn't go ahead with the evening as planned and let Mom hide in her room if she wanted. I hated to think of her up there alone while we partied within earshot. Since her arrival, she had yet to leave the house or see anyone except John and me.

"We can't keep putting our lives on hold," John said.

He was right. Our lives had to go on, especially now that Mom was moving-in. A shiver crept over my skin. I had yet to break that news.

Mom had overheard John and I argue. He reminded her of my father, she complained, so self-centered. With a pang, I recalled Dad's handsome, silver head thrown back, laughing. I hadn't spoken to him in almost two years, not since his split with Mom. He'd stopped phoning, but still wrote sometimes and sent regular emails. All of which I ignored. I didn't care that he was gay, although it felt weird, but I did care that he'd deceived us, deceived everyone, on so many levels and for so long. In the past, if I had made contact, it would have devastated Mom. Now, it would kill her.

Friday night, Carrie and Greg came over, punctual as ever. Carrie flashed her new braces and quipped that she'd have the perfect smile for her thirty-second birthday. She dipped a triangle of pita bread into the hummus and asked if she would get to see Mom, a giddy gleam in her eyes. I shot her a disgusted look, and she looked suitably chastened. The doorbell rang again. With everyone present, John blared The Eurythmics, and poured Cosmos all round.

Just as I'd cut the birthday cake, the phone rang. We ignored it. The caller persisted, phoned repeatedly. Eventually, I answered. It was Mom, on her cell phone. Stop the racket, she complained, her voice thick. I apologized and promised we'd quiet down.

I returned to the dining room, John telling everyone how terrible Mom looked.

Carrie touched her chest. "How awful."

"Stop, John," I snapped.

John shook his head, drunk already. "She's beyond recognizable."

"How dare you," I said.

I turned to the others. "It's temporary," I said, my voice faltering. "She'll get fixed."

"Nothing's going to undo that," he said.

"That's my mother you're talking about."

I looked around the table. Our guests shifted in their seats and avoided eye-contact.

"I'm sorry," John said. "I'm an idiot."

He topped everyone's drinks, and came and kissed the top of my head. "Sorry, babe."

I ignored him, but planned to give him hell as soon as everyone was gone.

He returned to his chair, and launched into a story about our eccentric garbage collector. The man claimed to have outfitted his entire house with gems he'd found at the city dump.

"He says, courtesy of the dump, he has the world's best porn collection." John bucked in his chair, his lips still greasy from the salmon.

The others erupted again, laughing hard.

Minutes later, from behind us, came Mom's choked voice. "For pity's sake, I'm trying to sleep."

Carrie's hand rushed to her mouth. John gaped. The others paled. I shot out of my chair. Mom stood in the doorway in her long white nightdress, ghostly and unsteady. Her wig was lop-sided and her make-up had melted. A doll burning in a fire. She looked from the others' repulsed expressions to me, her lips two wiggling worms. She made small, wounded noises.

I hurried to her, my arms out. "Mommy. It's okay, Mommy."

I led her back to the stairs. My lies echoed in the hall, came back at us. She felt so tiny inside my arm, fragile and childlike, and yet the burden of her slithered up my spine, tightened around my throat.

Scraps

The waitress brings her a glass of water with lemon. She wants red wine. It's too early for wine. She returns to *The Times* and scans the headlines: disasters, scandals, dead celebrities. There's a strong smell of rosemary. She checks the clock again and feels her heartbeat in her throat.

He arrives, dressed in a mustard-yellow raincoat. She checks the sky, the gray clouds still a long way off. If he can look like that, she can have wine. She signals the waitress. His cheeks are weather-beaten and brown sun spots mark his forehead. She looks down at the table. His car keys hit the small vase centerpiece and the legs of his chair screech across the tiles. He doesn't remove his raincoat. His dark, cracked hands make her think of tree bark. He meets her gaze and smirks. She sees a flash of him sucking her nipples. Her face grows hot and numb.

Beyond the window, a black Labrador big as a baby bear is tied to the bus stop pole. The dog sniffs passersby and complains low in his throat. The waitress takes their order, her accent Australian. He's come straight from the Botanical Gardens where he tends the tropical plants and smells of earth and green. His fingernails are broken black ecosystems. Once, they made love in the Gardens' greenhouse, hidden inside the forest of potted plants. It takes all her strength not to tell him to remove his coat and to go wash his hands.

They discuss the sale of the cottage, the only thing they had legally owned together. It is white-washed and covered in green moss and is the one place that feels like home; she wishes she could afford to buy him out. With his dirty fingernail, he pushes his slice of lemon into his soda. The previous night, mosquitoes had feasted on the backs of her legs. She struggles not to scratch at the raised bites, to not order a second glass.

He sucks on his lemon rind. They had met at a friend's fortieth birthday party, a casino on a boat in the Bay. In the last hand of the night, her house of queens beat his house of tens. Outside, a woman feeds the Lab from a greasy, brown paper bag. The dog's tail thumps the ground, the whisper of a jump-rope, and his eyelids droop with pleasure.

"How's that teen intern you're banging?" she asks. The word is foreign in her mouth, but satisfying.

"She's twenty," he says.

"Tell her I said 'Happy Birthday.'"

The waitress returns with the check on a white plate with three tiny cookies. His dirty hand paws all three. Down the back of the nursery is his tool chest, if he still keeps it there, and inside is a manicure set she'd included in his Christmas stocking. She has clipped his nails and rubbed his feet, kissed his toes.

She takes her copies of the paperwork and hurries into her coat. The food whirls in her stomach like a spinning top.

He remains seated, chews on the last cookie.

The bells of a nearby church ring-out and their peals shake the window in its frame. Storm clouds have gathered. The Labrador and woman walk off side by side. She steps into the street, gulps the charged air.

All There, Waiting

In the bedroom, inside the mural, there's a boy, park, red truck, and blue fish that fly in and out between the branches and about the boy's dark head. Also on the wall, the father can see faces where there are no faces: The boy his baby son would have become, the future man that will never be. Everywhere he looks—inside the wall, window, his palms and black leather toecaps—he sees his dead baby, just as he looked inside the tiny, but still too big, coffin.

Every now and then his wife passes by the open door and looks in at him like he's a fool. He is a fool. She is a fool. We are all fools. God is a fool. He is craving cheese. String cheese. Something he can peel and peel. He does not want to eat the cheese. He wants to smear the cheese on the mural, over the boy, park, fish, and truck.

When he was a boy, according to his mother, he couldn't say truck. He said fuck. He says fuck now, over and over. He calls to his wife, asks if they have string cheese. She shouts back, tells him to stop swearing, to get out of that bedroom. He asks for chips, salt and vinegar flavored. Something he can smash and crunch between his teeth. Bitter chips he can spit at the mural. Spit and smear. Bananas too. He wants bananas to mash and smear. Blacken. Rot.

"Fuck," he shouts.

"Truck," he shouts.

His wife charges up the stairs and into the room.

"Get up," she says. "Get up and get out. We can't do this anymore. We have to get on with our lives. It's what he would have wanted."

He is half-blind with temper. How do they know what he would have wanted? They didn't have him for nearly long enough. She takes off her wedding rings and fires them at his chest.

"Is this what you want?" she asks. "Do you want to kill everything?"

There, he thinks, it's said. He killed their baby. A screw goes through his right temple and into his brain, turns and turns.

There's a rippling movement on the wall, the same circles that flow out from a penny dropped in a wishing well. It is the boy moving in the mural, he realizes, cart-wheeling across the wall. He hears the boy spin through the air, hears his feet land in the grass, hears his ragged breath. His son would have grown to be fast and strong and brave. Happy. Imperfect. Great. He would never have stood still.

He scrambles to his feet, and mirrors the boy, cartwheels again and again. Fly, he tells his son, fly.

The Bridge They Said Couldn't Be Built

Ben caught my attention one foggy morning on the
Golden Gate Bridge, it clear at a glance that he was agitated
and overwrought. He paced back and forth next to the rail,
muttering and rubbing his face. I approached him as I would a
frothing dog. Several passersby looked at him twice, but no one
stopped. I hurried past, avoided eye contact. His pacing and
hand gestures turned frantic, and he let loose an anguished cry. I
doubled back, and asked if he needed help. He spat out a bitter
laugh.

I persisted, struck by his helpless boy face, his green eyes.
He moved toward the bridge rail, threatening to jump. I offered
to call someone, pulled my phone from my pocket. He licked
his lips, his eyes darting between the phone and the ocean, and
croaked numbers, his ex-wife's. I dialed her, the phone damp in
my hands. She refused to speak with him. I stared at the dead
phone, incredulous. Ben faced the ocean and gripped the bridge
rail.

I peeled my tongue from the roof of my mouth. "You want
to go get a beer?"

He shook his head hard and seemed more appalled by beer
than suicide.

"You can always come back later?" I coaxed. "The fog will

have burned off and you can go out in far more spectacular surroundings."

His thick eyebrows climbed. "I don't drink."

"Maybe that's your problem."

He flexed the barest smile.

I babbled, told him about the fresh doughnuts in my car. I was parked real close, right at the start of the bridge.

"These doughnuts are so good you just might die from ecstasy alone, save the theatrics—"

He shook his head. "You're crazy."

I didn't state the obvious.

We were almost at my car. I could tell he was wavering, that his skeleton was turning inside his skin, twisting back toward the ocean.

I resumed my jabber. "They serve these doughnuts still warm from the oven, taste like they're from a fairy tale."

My car smelled of a bakery, of spices from the air freshener. Ben's teeth sank into the jam-filled doughnut, and his eyes widened as the flavors hit. He licked sugar from his lips and jam from the edges of his mouth. I tucked into the second doughnut, and enjoyed it far more than felt right. I licked my chin, catching chocolate and ocean salt.

I told Ben how I liked to walk the Bridge every Sunday morning, liked how the wind sifted through me, how the fog swallowed me.

"Do you think there's a heaven?" he asked.

"Here, this is heaven."

"This is hell," he said.

"It's that too."

He told me how he and Shirley had broken-up after five years of marriage. How she'd thought he had no backbone. He was going to show her. He'd never fit right in the world, he went on. He'd always felt lonely, out of step. He was done trying.

I grasped at the right things to say. He remained distracted and stared back at the bridge. I asked if there was someone else he could call. He demanded Shirley, again. I hesitated, another wave of adrenalin coursing through me. I pushed the worst from my mind. Perhaps she'd talk to him this time, get through to him.

"Please," he said.

I dialed, trembling. Shirley hung-up again. Ben held his head. I thought to dial 9-1-1, but he would have cleared the bridge before the dispatcher even had time to answer.

Ben clutched his stomach. "I'm going to be sick."

He leaned out the passenger door and retched.

The smells of vomit and fear took over the car. I considered driving to a police station or the hospital, but decided he would bolt as soon as I parked or might even jump en route from the moving car.

"Please let me take you to the hospital." My voice sounded too high and quivery.

He rushed from the car. I charged after him, shouting.

He finally stopped, at much the same spot where we'd met less than an hour earlier.

We watched the water, sailboats, seagulls, and Alcatraz in silence. Seals clamored over the far rocks, barked. We hugged ourselves against the encroaching fog.

I tried again. "You can't do this. This is insane."

He rested his head on his arms on the rail.

I thought of my father dead from lung cancer, my mother alive but lost to Alzheimer's, and my brother wooden with depression, people I couldn't save no matter how hard I'd tried.

"Right," I said. "Let's both jump." I moved to the rail. I

meant it, in that moment I really meant it.

He tugged on my arm. "I know what you're trying to do. It's not going to work."

"I'm serious, I'll jump too."

"That's just stupid."

"I'm stupid? You're stupid. You really think your life's so worthless? You think you can just check-out? What about the rest of us?" I slapped my chest. "We play by the rules even when we don't want to, when it's hard and it hurts, unbearable. We go on even as we worry we'll never be anything close to happy. What about us?"

I pulled myself up onto the bridge and swung my legs over the rail, dangled above the ocean. "So let's go. Let's do it." My heart thumped in my throat.

Ben grabbed at my waist and pulled me backwards into his arms. I slapped at him. "Don't you touch me. And don't you dare stand there and tell me it's not okay for me to jump, but it's okay for you. Who made you so special?" My voice broke.

He grabbed at his hair and made helpless, wounded noises.

I pushed my face close to his. "Go ahead. Do whatever you want."

I forced myself toward my car, my breath uneven and legs iron. He wouldn't jump. I knew he wouldn't jump. A minute passed. Two. Three. I was just about to turn around when his shouts reached me.

The whole drive home, I thought I must be just as crazy as Ben. In my apartment, he wanted nothing more than to sleep. Like a baby, he said, like he hadn't a care. He offered to take the couch, but I insisted he sleep in my bed. Too tired to take off his clothes, he fell in between the clean sheets and pulled the blankets up to his chin. I moved a chair to the side of the bed and watched while he slept. He lay on his side, his hands in prayer under his cheek. His eyes darted behind his lids.

On my dresser stood the gold-framed photograph of my parents and my broken brother. I tasted salt, and again heard the seagulls. Often, I, too, didn't feel able for this world. Sometimes, even leaving my apartment proved too much. Some days, I didn't think I'd make it through. I relived those moments on the bridge rail when I'd leaned over the water and stared into its green, blue, silver, and golden hues, its gleam—terrified, tempted.

Far From Angels

After her mother died, Sarah believed she would never again be able to sleep. Every time she closed her eyes, she saw a white beast with red eyes and black fangs coming for her, just as it had come for her mother. The cancer, first feasting on her mother's right breast, wouldn't be sated and tore right through her.

Sarah's maternal grandmother insisted on attending the funeral. Sarah did not want to meet this woman she'd never known. Her name, when rarely mentioned, was met with silence and dark expressions. As soon as the adults learned of her grandmother's imminent arrival, they puffed their cheeks and spat out *why bother.* A few placed bets on how long she'd stay sober.

Grandmother descended with twig limbs and a head like an egg, tiny inside her black blouse and skirt. Sarah's father greeted his mother-in-law with the same stiffness he reserved for the priest and the funeral parlor director. The last time they'd spoken was at his shotgun wedding. She'd disowned them before passing out on the hotel lawn. Now she presented Sarah with a rainbow-swirl lollipop almost as big as the eleven-year-old's face.

After the introductions, Sarah disappeared to her bedroom

and tossed the lollipop into the garbage can. She stretched out on her bed, much like her mother in her coffin. She closed her eyes and saw the beast. Her eyes flew open. She stared down her t-shirt at her breast buds and recalled the white spots on her mother's x-rays.

Grandmother appeared, startling her. She perched on the edge of Sarah's bed, her teeth the color of corn. The ice cubes in her brandy glass knocked together. Sarah wrinkled her nose at the alcohol's tang, but liked the way the sunlight danced in its amber shades. Her grandmother narrowed her rheumy eyes and complained that the people downstairs were singing folk songs when they should be praying.

Birdsong carried into the room. Grandmother mumbled something about the bees killing the birds. She downed her drink, her mouth a nozzle, and stopped short of the dredges. Sarah felt sharp pains in her hands, like needles going under her fingernails. She wished she was dead, with her mother. Grandmother's small eyes found the tossed lollipop. Sarah looked away. The old woman told her she'd eaten an entire sirloin steak on the flight, washed it down with red wine.

Grandmother pushed the brandy close to Sarah's mouth and ordered her to drink. Sarah pulled back from the greasy glass. The witch laughed. Sarah shuddered at her grandmother's hot breath, its sour, wilted smell. Grandmother stared into the last of the drink, her shriveled lips pursed. She asked if her daughter had ever talked about her. Sarah shook her head.

"Never?" she asked.

"Never," Sarah said.

She asked if she'd told Sarah about her grandfather. Sarah nodded.

Her grandmother sniffed, *yes, she made a hero out of him.*

She exited the room on shaky legs, her egg-head trembling.

Sarah yawned, and despite herself, closed her eyes. She saw her grandmother's head tremble, tremble and topple right off her shoulders. It rolled across the floor and out into the hall. Sarah didn't even try to catch it.

The Long Way

Harry points his forehead and pleads with his soft blue eyes. The latest band he's following, Dewdrops, are playing downtown at eight. I tell him that going to these concerts and trying to network with these singers and musicians won't further his career any. Only making music will. His eyes keep asking.

It's another small nightclub with too many speakers and not enough ventilation, too dark in places, in others too bright, glaring. The crowd presses against us, screams and jumps, sloshes drinks. The beat works up through our feet and collides in our chests. There's also the surge from the magic brownies. It occurs to me that Dewdrops's lead singer is Spock, the two guitarists Bones and Scotty, and the drummer Captain Kirk. Harry and I pull on the tops of our ears and push up our eyebrows, shout *Star Trek* catch phrases. It's impossible to stand straight. We dance, shriek, *"I'm giving her all she's got, Captain."*

There's a long line in the restroom. I cross my legs and struggle not to leak. Women talk and laugh. From inside the last cubicle, someone retches, and groans. *Beam me up, Scotty.* I don't trust my bladder enough to allow myself to laugh. After I use the restroom, I wash my hands and splash my face. Next to me, two girls preen in the mirror and re-touch their make-up.

They gush and giggle about the lead singer. The blond says he's a bottle of cold beer, a longneck. Says she knows just what to do with him. They cackle, show the dark pink holes of their throats. I cup cool water in my palms, and sip. Water is so huge, so necessary, and I'm holding it right here in my hands. *Fascinating.* Something between a giggle and a groan escapes my throat, and the girls eye me, their upper lips pulled back, as thin and pale as deli ham. I stop at the bathroom door and tell them he's no bottle of beer, he's Spock, dammit, Spock.

After the concert, Harry and I wait for the band to reappear and give autographs. We drink the last of our warm beer and cling to feeling high. Harry parts with our hard-earned money and buys another CD, one more to add to the multi-colored stacks in our living room. Last year, I gave up on alphabetical order. Harry hands the CD to Spock for his autograph and tells him about his music, his hopes. Spock bobs his head and scribbles. His eyes jump to the blond behind us, the girl from the bathroom. Harry talks faster, hustles. Spock's no longer listening. The blond sidles next to Harry and jostles him out of her way. Her stilettos cut fresh holes in the carpet. Spock gives her a most un-Vulcan like smile. I want to hurt them.

"It'll happen," I tell Harry again on the walk home, believing it a little less every time.

He squeezes my hand, "You bet it'll happen."

Dewdrops's beat goes around in my head, still holds me. I feel an insane need for food, for the music to stop.

Harry hugs me. "My big break's coming. I can feel it." I look down at the cracked pavement. He pulls me toward the subway. I pretend to be still high and as we go underground shout, *"To the transporter."*

At home, Harry plays his new CD, and reaches for me. We taste of sweet and sour from the two-day old Chinese. The

take-out cartons lie scattered about the blue carpet. Icebergs.
Harry moves on top of me and grunts in time to Captain Kirk's
drums. I get up and turn off the music. Harry protests, and then
humors me. He sings his latest song, the chorus about kissing
the sky. After, we arch and curve, knot and buck, damp, salty.

I watch Harry sleep, his face bathed in moonlight and
our breaths synchronized. He dreams so much while awake
I wonder that there's anything left for sleep. His lips form a
straight red line, seem to mock us.

The Trip

Dad insisted on the vacation to Galway and badgered me into going along. He had visited Ireland twice before, as a boy and a young man, and now this trip at age seventy-five. I wondered again how I—out of his five children—got saddled with him. Mother, in a rare show of defiance, refused to make the journey, too frail, too smart.

Shortly after the plane took off, Dad jumped out of his seat, shouting. He insisted he'd seen a rat dart out from the cockpit and disappear under the seats. Crew and passengers stared while I tried to calm him. I spiked a coca-cola with two of his sleeping tablets. He slept through the rest of the flight like a babe.

The ruddy-faced immigration official looked up from our American passports with a small smile. "Here to trace your roots?"

Dad shot back in his leprechaun brogue. "I'm one hundred percent Irish and know my roots already, thanks very much."

The official cocked an eyebrow, amused. "Is that so?"

I'd read The Xenophobes Guide on the flight, and learned that the Irish scoffed at Yanks who claimed they were Irish. If you weren't born and bred, forget it.

Dad pushed back his curved shoulders. "Both sets of

grandparents were from the old sod."

The official and I shared a conspiratorial smile. He waved us on.

In baggage claim, Dad demanded my phone. He wanted to gloat to Patrick, the eldest, inform him that we'd arrived. I handed the phone over and warned him not to talk for too long, the cost. He punched two buttons on the phone and pressed it to his large ear. I checked my temper and explained that the speed dials he used on his home phone wouldn't work from my phone, and certainly not from Ireland.

He stared at me, flabbergasted. "What do you mean it won't work? Patrick's star five." His voice climbed. "He's always been star five."

People turned to look.

We walked to our rental car, the wind slicing at us. I pushed the laden baggage cart, and Dad hobbled behind, muttering.

When he saw our rental car, a red hatchback, he balked. "I'm not getting into that."

He wanted a green car. I coaxed and bullied him, but he wouldn't budge. He suffered from a green fixation, as out of control as any addict. Everything in his house, inside and out, was green, right down to the kitchen appliances and the bathroom fixtures. If an item couldn't be had in green, he painted it over. Much to Mother's horror, he had even painted sea-green the statue of the Virgin Mary in the transom over their front door. The family joke was that his meds were "anti-greens."

The Hertz employee apologized again, there were no green cars available.

Dad shouted. "What kind of a racket are you running here?"

I half-dragged, half-carried him off.

We were on the road at last, Dad still sulking. I might have enjoyed the quiet if it wasn't for the cold blast that howled through his open window. Despite the chill October day, he insisted on keeping his window down. Only when we were well clear of the airport and surrounded by lush pastures, grazing livestock, and farmhouses with smoke billowing from their chimneys did his mood brighten.

"The forty shades of green." He sucked rudely at the air, as if to ingest every hue.

We stopped into a pub for lunch. Dad located the public pay phone. He wanted to call Mom, anxious to know how his Alsatians, Eileen and Maureen, were faring without him. I bought him a phone card, and dialed. From the back of the pub I could hear him shout into the phone, as if trying to be heard through a blizzard.

"How's Eimeen? You taking good care of them? They miss me?" He shouted.

Dad never got names right and relished mixing and morphing them.

"Put Eimeen on the phone. I said to just put them on already."

My face and ears warmed. I smiled like I didn't know him.

Hours later, we were still trapped inside the car. We had gotten lost and delayed in traffic. The greasy beef stew Dad had insisted on for lunch repeated on me and heartburn tore up my chest.

Dad's words of comfort? "Better than your mother's though, wasn't it?"

We neared a white-washed, thatched pub, its windows flooded with light the cast of daffodils. Traditional music carried through Dad's open window. He wanted to stop, have a pint of Guinness. Exhausted, I tried to reason with him. It made far more sense to continue to our hotel and get settled for the night. We were both up for eighteen hours and counting. He waved away my protests and upbraided me with another of his war stories. He'd served as a merchant marine in World War II and with the U.S. Army in Korea. In Korea, at the 38th Parallel North, for three nights and three days straight he had lain in a trench, his finger pressed to the trigger of his rifle, terrified to even blink. To lose his focus or to fall asleep meant death, if not from enemy fire then hypothermia.

"So don't boo-hoo me about jetlag," he finished.

I turned the car around.

We entered the dingy pub, its air choked with blue-gray cigarette smoke. An army of musicians sat around the open fire, its yellow-orange flames licking the blackened chimney. Dad pushed his way through the throng to the bar. People shot annoyed looks. I followed him, apologizing. He didn't consult with me, just went ahead and ordered two pints of Guinness, and hurried off to the bathroom. I watched how the barman poured the stout. Moments later, Dad reappeared at the opposite end of the bar and beckoned the barman. What now? The barman followed Dad back toward the bathrooms. Minutes later, he returned to work, but there was still no sign of Dad.

I purchased the drinks, and waited. The creamy head on Dad's pint started to brown. I found him flat on his back in the men's bathroom, his head and torso under the sink, fixing a leaky pipe. The smell of corroded metal snagged my breath, the pipe broken for quite some time. Why did I feel surprised? Dad always managed to find something that needed tinkering, but in the second pub we walked into in a foreign country? He ignored me, intent on his task. I returned to the bar.

Dad curled out his bottom lip when I refused to stay for a second pint of Guinness. I reminded him that I was driving in a strange country on the opposite side of treacherous roads that were as narrow and crooked as the bridge of his nose. Again he ignored me, and, to the great delight of all in the pub, broke into "Galway Bay." I'd never heard him sing. He sounded good, gifted even. When he finished, the place erupted with clapping, cheering, and whistling. The barman brought Dad a pint of Guinness, and patted his back.

As arranged, the next day we drove from the hotel to Dad's cousin's house. Our host, Robbie, pumped our hands—his own paw callused from decades of farm work and harsh weather. No matter how many times I corrected him, Dad called Robbie "Bobby." At least Robbie didn't seem to mind.

He marveled at how much I looked like Dad. "The mirror image."

I smiled tightly.

Inside the kitchen, Robbie's wife and daughter joined us for tea. Dad scowled across the table at the daughter and immediately I thought of his meds, back in the wash bag in the hotel, untouched since we'd left home. What was I thinking? The daughter was sixteen or so with rosy skin, black pixie hair, and large blue eyes. Rattled by Dad's hot stare, her cheeks grew redder and her body shrank lower in the chair.

His gruff voice startled us. "Where's all her hair?"

Robbie and his family exchanged looks.

"Don't you know the fashions nowadays?" Robbie's wife smiled uncertainly. "They'll do anything."

I tried to distract Dad, asked him which counties his grandparents hailed from, what year they'd emigrated. Dad suddenly leaned to his left, ducked his head under the table.

Our eyes widened. His muffled voice sounded, seemed to address the daughter again.

"Good, you're wearing shoes at least."

He reappeared, his face flushed.

I closed my eyes and chided myself. I knew better than to let his meds lapse. We got through the next half hour somehow, our Irish relatives growing more and more uncomfortable with each of Dad's outbursts.

"You hunt?" he asked Robbie.

Robbie's face knitted. "For the foxes?"

Dad smacked the table, making us jump. "No, not some sissy chase on horses. I mean with guns. You shoot birds? Deer?"

Robbie shifted in his chair. "No, none of that."

Dad looked wildly about the room. "You don't keep guns?"

Robbie laughed. "No, no, nothing like that."

"You need to get yourself a gun, man, protect your wife and family, your home."

"That's enough, Dad."

I smiled apologetically at our hosts. Robbie looked at his watch. I took his cue and thanked them. I ushered Dad out. At the door, he launched into "Galway Bay."

"Come on, Dad."

He sang on.

Robbie slapped his shoulder and led him to the car. He waved us off. The mother and daughter had stayed inside. Inside the car, I tuned the radio to country music, and Dad quieted.

I somehow survived the next five days of the trip, slipping Dad his meds with varying degrees of success. We completed whirlwind visits to distant relatives, the graves of our ancestors, and countless pubs that served suspect food and played traditional music. The one thing I really wanted to do was to travel to the Aran Islands, but Dad refused to join me.

"I'm not getting on any boat."

He was a Merchant Marine, for Christ's sake.

"It's a ferry," I corrected.

He remained stubborn.

I went anyway, and left him behind at the hotel. I had once asked my paternal grandmother if it was the wars that had made Dad so mean and crazy.

She'd laughed. "He was always that way."

I returned from the Aran Islands, an afternoon's adventure despite the rain, cold, and bruised sky. Inside the hotel's parking lot, I stopped short, disbelieving. I ran at our rental car. A woman pulling a bright pink suitcase stopped to gape. I touched the roof of our car, the paint still wet, my fingertips coming away hunter green. Dad had painted every inch of the vehicle, save the windows. Even the exhaust.

I charged into our hotel room, found Dad slouched in a chair at the window, his back to me. He didn't look around. I rushed at him, quaking with temper, but stopped, stunned. He had also painted his front hunter green, from his forehead down to his bare feet. He looked up at me, his glazed eyes loose in his head and mouth working hard, like he couldn't draw air.

I touched his wet shoulder. "It's okay, Dad. It's okay."

"I ... I ... I," he spluttered, till the words turned to strangled gasps.

Once he quieted, I carried a wet, warm towel from the bathroom, and started with his feet, careful, gentle.

Babies on the Shore

Just as I reached the beach, it rained. I tipped back my head. Raindrops stuck to my lips and turned to syrup in my gloss. Mother's ghost warned me to go back, that I would catch my death. I laughed—as if death was to be chased. I pressed on, the rain welcoming me. Mother said it was spitting at me. If we must walk, she sulked. She wanted to put the rain back in the sky, believed that she had the power. I sipped the rain, and rejoiced in how there were no cracks in the sand. The rain tasted sweet and savory at once, a cocktail. Mother said I would perish. I assured her, in a sarcastic drawl, that I was willing to sacrifice myself. She threatened to find a prescription for me yet.

Thousands of ladybugs dotted the shore, as though the ocean had just birthed them. See, I told Mother, ladybugs were a good omen. They're dead, she said. They weren't. I tried to insert a tender finger into a raindrop. I wondered what was inside, what had it got? There you go again, Mother said, with your funny ideas. Her words tattooed me. The rain kissed me. In the distance, a long white sailboat sat on the water. Boats, ocean currents, its creatures, they all frightened me. Mother scoffed, said you always were afraid.

The shower turned heavy. Did rain have memory, know where it ended and began? Who felt abandoned, the rain or the clouds? Did rain ever suffer fear, sadness, anger? Was it ever happy? Mother laughed, harsh. I asked the rain for its hand, just as I had often asked my father for his. When I didn't feel its pull, I lifted my head to the sky and wished the rain would liquidate me, take me into itself. From behind me, Mother said, would you stop.

I whirled around, knowing she was both there and not there. The rain has color, Mom. Can you see that? Can you hear rain sing? Feel rain hold you. She said the rain was impotent, baby drool. Have you ever danced with the rain, Mom? Tasted rain? Talked with rain? Did she know that rain was something to be opened, drop by drop? She shook her head, refused to look at me. I wanted to smack her, to hear the splat that a water balloon makes when it bursts. Only when I looked again, I realized that mixed with the rain, her downcast face was wet with tears, drop after drop falling.

Found and Lost

I was at the office, typing at my desk, when the baby materialized on my lap. She sat upright and was bald, naked, and drooling. Her dappled fist rammed into her pink mouth. The back of her head pushed against my breasts.

My boss and coworkers demanded an explanation. I had no idea. She couldn't be my manifestation. I wasn't barren or childless. I had too many children. I phoned the police and Child Services. *Finders keepers,* they said and hung-up.

I purchased diapers, baby rice, and a onesie, all while balancing the baby on my hip. She gurgled, generating saliva bubbles and wetting my shirt. Anyone fool enough to coo and gush, I pushed right past.

I arrived home. When my daughter and youngest son saw the baby, they groaned and slapped the furniture. The oldest shrieked *not again.* I placed the baby on the floor, and kneaded the ache in my lower back. The children pulled their feet clear whenever she crawled close. I asked if they had a hand in her appearance, if they knew who did. They denied everything.

My husband appeared and slapped his briefcase onto the kitchen table. Our oldest suggested we house the baby outside in the dog kennel until we could get her gone. My husband cocked his eyebrow, half-tempted. We decided against. Bruce might eat her. The baby cried. My breasts leaked. I sighed, and raised my shirt. She made grunting, slurping sounds at my nipple. I felt a scraping sensation at the back of my throat.

I pulled out the bottom drawer of our bedroom dresser and arranged a crib of sorts. In bed, my husband and I argued and blamed. I obviously wanted another kid, he accused. He was the anal-retentive one, I shot back, liked even numbers. She's your angst, he insisted. Yours, I said. We turned our backs to each other, and tug-o-warred for the blankets. The baby cried and cried. I nursed her again, and exhausted, allowed her to sleep between us.

The next morning, she had vanished. I searched and searched, to no avail. Once it became clear she was gone, our family never mentioned her again, but our stops and stares and withdrawal into ourselves gave our doubts and paranoia away. Even Bruce fell under suspicion. I sold our bedroom dresser and bed, but the baby's memory persisted, her warmth, sounds, and smells, her tight fists, large eyes cut from the sky, and hair like a crow's wing.

"What baby?" I told the children. "There wasn't any baby."

The walls and ceilings in our house advanced on us, its air sickened and emptied. The furniture and trappings morphed into fingers that pointed and jabbed. Five of us left to wonder ever after who had caused the baby to appear, then disappear, and why? How?

Vitals

Whenever people met my mother, they half-bowed and shook her hand for too long, said, "Doctor Duke's wife, well, well." I was Doctor Duke's son, with his shock of dark curly hair and too small face, the boy headed for high places. When I was real small I imagined that meant I'd climb to the top of the purple mountain range I could see from our kitchen window.

Mother, fair and slight, always wore a house apron. I remember most the one covered with large golden daffodils and long dark stems. The flowers growing up that apron, going to smother her one day.

Doctor Duke liked "supper at six sharp." That's how he talked, sounded like a hand-saw cutting through wood. When I laughed at more of his silly orders, asking Mother to please wear make-up at the supper table, he said he'd knock me into the dark with ether if I didn't watch myself. For hours after, I stared into our bathroom mirror.

Saturday mornings, when Doctor Duke had left for his practice and I didn't have school, I'd climb into his and mother's bed and lie in his big dip in the mattress, sinking. Mother smelled of that oatmeal face cream she wore at night. I wondered what Doctor Duke smelled like first thing in the mornings. Mother would mock-snore and puff out her pale pink lips with her breath, always giving up the game because we'd get to giggling so hard.

Once, her eyes still closed, she asked me to check her pulse. I didn't want to play. I wouldn't ever be a doctor. Please, she urged. I lifted her hand into mine, surprised that it felt smaller, rougher, than just the previous day. I held my first two fingers to her wrist, too squeamish to look at the dark blue veins.

"Well?" she asked.

"Sshh. I'm counting."

"I'm here, though?" she whispered. "Tell me I'm here."

The Key

They eloped to Rome and avoided the expense of a reception, the fuss and spectacle. She had all that fanfare a decade ago, the first time around. Pope Benedict XVI didn't make eye contact. She chased his bright, green eyes, but he wouldn't be caught. She felt she was back on the airplane, experiencing turbulence. Her groom winked at her. She was forty-five, he was thirty-four.

Earlier that afternoon, they had plucked two witnesses, strangers, from outside a café and bribed the gorgeous couple. During the ceremony, the olive-skinned woman betrayed them with a barely suppressed smirk, mirrored the hot whispers and crude jokes of so many back home in Bridgeport, Connecticut. She was a widow turned cradle snatcher.

Outside the Basilica, the lanky, too-thin photographer repeated *bella* as she pressed her rouged cheek against her new husband's. She smiled from her toes up, much of her high mood restored. After, they dined at The Ponte Milvio, renowned for its food, romantic ambience, and a certain lovers' ritual.

He reached across the narrow table for her hand. They smiled into each other. In recent weeks he'd grown a thick mustache, black wiry hair spliced with ginger that made his kisses saltier. His brown eyes held hints of red. Pink-cheeked, he looked permanently flushed. He'd bulked-up too, his body harder, its smell more potent. She wondered if he realized that he didn't just look older, but more and more like her first husband, Brian.

She sipped her iced water. No matter how hard she tried not to, her eyes returned to the new pimple on his chin, red and bloodied. He grinned and squeezed her hand. She reached for the menu. He watched her struggle to decipher the small print, offered to read the menu aloud. Some time soon, she would have to give in to reading glasses. She said she'd have whatever he was having.

"You're smarter than that," he said.

A vein throbbed in her jaw. Brian would never have killed the moment, not on such an occasion. Again that sensation of sharp pecks on her back. She needed to stop comparing the two men.

They clinked champagne glasses and toasted to a long and happy life together, to health and good fortune. They swore they would never become dull. Never, she repeated. He enjoyed the venison and she the sea bass. During dessert, strawberry cheesecake that sickened her slightly, four violinists serenaded them with Beethoven's "Ode to Joy." Heartened, she pulled her new husband out of his chair. They waltzed, their bodies pressed together, warm and damp. The other patrons murmured, clapped. The meal over, they made their way outside, the air cool and sun setting.

The restaurant was famous for its padlock ceremony, a ritual where couples placed a lock around one of the three lamp posts and threw the key into the river, wished for their love to always be safe. While the waiter, patrons, and passersby looked-on, she and her new husband attached the silver padlock to the first lamp post, and moved to the bridge, tossed the key into the brown river. People clapped and cheered. The newlyweds hugged and kissed, and waved goodbye.

They strolled arm-in-arm through the dark cobblestone streets, the way lit only by the moon and odd lantern. He whispered into her ear, his breath tepid and laced with cognac, *I would see you even in the pitch dark.* They stopped, kissed long and deep, their mouths strawberry sweet. She also tasted her guilt, and regretted her irritation and dark thoughts earlier. She was the moon and this man her sun, the light that shone through her. She had believed that she would never again find such love.

Pope Benedict's fervent whispers came back to her, his Latin prayers a mystery, but vibrating with that universal *and please and please and please.* A feeling of dread took hold of her and for a terrible moment she wanted to kick off her shoes and race back through the streets, to the river, and the key at its dark, silt bottom. She should have kept the key close-at-hand always, whispered into it her fears and hopes.

He walked backwards up the hill, tugging her by both hands, laughing. "Come, come."

She followed, prayed.

Fish

My older sister drives and I listen to her prattle on, everything outside just as drab—the trees, red barns, and stone houses. So much road kill. We turn a corner and plow through yellow, orange, and red leaves. In the rearview mirror, I watch the brittle leaves hover and swirl, and fall again. I want to jump out and run back, to curl up small beneath the pile.

We stall in traffic in a fast food drive-thru. She can't see what I find so funny. Drive-thru, I repeat and shake my head and look out my too clean window and think how I'm about to eat a quarter pound of dead cow. My mouth sours.

We're back on the road. She talks faster, and speeds the car to our mother. I ask why we have to watch Mom die. Hear her last breaths. Hold her impossibly blue hands. Didn't we see her enough? My sister looks at me in horror, but she knows that I am part right, that it's tempting to turn the car around.

On and on she talks, constant as the too-low radio. *Remember when …*

Soon, in the hospital, we will have to turn off Mom's life support. Little trip, I say aloud and laugh again. My sister slaps the back of my hand. It smarts. She'd left her three-year-old, Danielle, with her sitter, told her we were just going on a little trip. A single mother, she'd gotten pregnant just out of high

85

school and thinks she has to protect Danielle from everything, especially hard truths. Some part of me is still back there with Danielle, on the swings.

I never liked driving and won't get behind the wheel unless it's the last resort. I'm afraid I will get lost, or maimed, or killed in a crash. I want a quick, painless death, thank you, in my bed in my sleep. Just like we're going to give Mom. We drive and drive, and it feels like it's taking forever. Like we're driving clear through the county, the state, and the next state and the next, and I wonder just how far we'd have to go to be out of states and hospitals and dying mothers.

We enter the hospital parking garage. There's a slurping sound and I turn and see that my sister looks just like our mother did forty years ago. Right down to the three red splotches that break out under her left eye whenever there are tears. Oh, no, not crying. Where will crying get us? Get us enough water for fish is where, and fish stink. That's what our mother always said when we were little.

The hospital's gray machines whirr and bleep. Fish stink rises. My sister and I nod in unison. The nurses unplug the respirator and roll it away. Its wheels squeak over the linoleum, feel like they're running over my chest.

Across the corridor, in another room, a patient is propped against her pillows. A man with blond hair and a shiny navy suit leans in close. On her lap, stunning orange roses. I go to leave. The nurse with the black-brown mole next to her nose tells me there isn't time.

I stay, but in my mind I run. I run through the squeaky corridors and outside and chase from street to street, my shoes kicked-off and a stabbing pain in my throat. I search and search, and would drive, fly, swim, vault—anything—to return to my mother with glorious orange roses, twelve thorny babies in my arms that I hold out to her and say, Look, Mommy. See, Mommy. Aren't they gorgeous, Mommy? Touch, Mommy. Smell, Mommy. Breathe, Mommy. Beautiful Mommy. Breathe.

Rattle

Gary opens his front door to find a young man standing on his step, the stranger well muffled-up in a navy scarf and camel-colored duffel coat. Right off, Gary notices something familiar. The man is tall and broad, good-looking, ordinary enough but for his startling blue eyes. Gary tenses. The blue of his daughter's, Jane's, eyes. Darren introduces himself. Jane had named him something else.

Gary invites him in, and calls upstairs to his wife, Lily. He leads Darren into the kitchen. Darren can't know it, but he chooses the chair Jane always sits in. Gary boils the kettle for tea. His hands shake. Lily somehow knows Darren immediately. She attempts to hug him. Darren's arms remain at his sides. Gary fusses with mugs and teabags. He can no longer reach the china cups, his shoulders seized with arthritis. Lily searches the bottom cupboards for biscuits, anything sweet.

Darren lowers his spoon to the table, his nails manicured. He asks about his mother. Jane lives nearby and is married with three—Gary catches himself—other children, all girls.

Darren's jaw juts to the left.

Lily reappears, her arms loaded with thick photo albums. She and Darren pore over the photographs. She laughs where she can. Darren says little. Gary cannot look. That his fourteen-year-old daughter had given herself to a man still makes him want to scratch himself till he bleeds. Darren taps the large photograph taken when Jane turned twenty-one, a black-and-white close-up of her in a bee-hive and pearl drop earrings. She looks like a movie-star. Darren asks if he can have the photograph. Lily hesitates, she loves that picture. She disappears to find an envelope, for the photo's safekeeping.

Left alone, the two men are silent. Gary thinks he can hear a jackhammer in the distance. He asks about the drive over, if there was much construction. Darren shakes his head, like he couldn't care less.

"They're forever fixing the roads around here." Gary smiles. "I think they put in more potholes than they fill, to give themselves work."

Darren stares at the kitchen door. Gary cringes inside.

Lily reappears. She places the photograph inside the large brown envelope and hands it to Darren. He stands, and gives her a square of yellow paper with his contact information. At the front door, Darren ignores Gary's outstretched hand. The defiant thrust of his jaw channels Jane.

Lily touches Darren's arm. "You'll come again?"

The doctor had taken Darren away immediately after the birth, said that was best. Gary recalls the silver rattle Jane had given to the nurses, wonders if they ever passed it along to the adoptive family. He sees a flash of Darren still sleeping with the rattle under his pillow, of his putting it on a chain and wearing it around his neck by day. His eyes jump to the bulge of scarf at Darren's chest. For years, Jane had nightmares. Said she heard that silver rattle in her sleep, loud, incessant, that her ears bled and bled. Darren moves down the front path. Lily throws sprinkles of holy water after him.

Cracking Open

Her addiction started with dry roasted nuts, and quickly jumped to peanuts. At her worst, she was consuming a large glass jar of peanuts daily. She loved and yet hated their salty taste and greasy feel, the repetition of tossing them into her mouth.

"You're making a monkey out of yourself, and me," her husband said.

Her weight nudged three hundred pounds. She couldn't afford therapy and had no success with Weight Watchers. Instead, she attended local Alcoholics Anonymous meetings and inwardly substituted "peanuts" in all the pertinent places.

After several weeks, she abandoned AA, too weird. She substituted the peanuts with shelled nuts, lower in fat and calories, and limited herself to a cup or two a day. Happier, she especially enjoyed the messy process of cracking open the fibrous shells and fishing out the shriveled nuts. Her husband complained about the litter of shells and dust throughout the house. She took to gluing the shells to the kitchen appliances, and sticking them to the walls and furniture.

"You've turned our home into a monkey house," he said.

One Saturday morning, he appeared in the kitchen, a suitcase hanging from each arm.

In a rage, she jumped up and down. The house quaked and its contents teetered. Most of the peanut shells fell to the ground. She jumped and jumped, and sprang her skinny self out of her carcass.

Her husband dropped the suitcases and reached for her. "Baby, you're back."

She pushed him away. "Take the peanuts when you go."

She whirled around, and side-kicked her enormous husk full in the chest. The husk crashed to the floor. Its reverberations shook the glued shells from the walls, from the furniture and appliances, and they, too, fell to the floor. She lifted the shells and tossed them up into the air, laughed as they showered her. Her husband gaped, a mannequin. She danced from room to room, as naked and loud as the day she was born.

At the Peephole

I parked outside Eddie's redbrick apartment building and skulked inside my end-stage Honda Civic, working up the courage. The car windows fogged. I checked my reflection in the rearview mirror and removed my black beanie. It made my face too round. The wind picked up right as my sneakers hit the tarmac. I reached into the backseat for the pink and purple donkey piñata, and then slipped inside the building behind the Greek-looking pizza guy.

Mrs. Jacobsen from twelve-seventeen passed us on her way out. She looked twice at the piñata, but didn't recognize me. Up until seven weeks ago, we were neighbors, for over two years. The pizza guy and I rode the too-small elevator in silence. He didn't as much as glance at me or the donkey. I could smell sausage and pineapple, his sweat and pomade. He exited on ten. Used to be, no guy could stay around me that long without starting something.

The elevator stopped on twelve with a clang. The doors opened. I froze. The doors started to close. I pressed the hold button. The elevator alarm went-off, much like a donkey's bray. I pushed out, the piñata heavy now, its crepe paper damp against my hands.

Eddie's familiar footfall sounded behind the apartment door. I sensed him at the peephole. The donkey felt enormous and ridiculous against my chest. Eddie finally appeared, his t-shirt tight on his muscles, his blond hair mussed, and those topaz eyes. He looked back and forth between the donkey and me. My mouth opened, but the words didn't form. I pushed the piñata into his arms. He made some astonished gasp. I had filled the donkey with stones, measured the weight to fifteen pounds, exactly how much more there was of me now.

"An ass for an ass," I said.

"Let's not do this—"

"I'm breaking-up with you."

He shook his head, his eyes animal sad.

My face warmed. "What? Because you say we're over that's supposed to be it? I don't have a say? I don't think so. I'm here to finish with you. Now we're over."

His eyes darted up and down the corridor. "You're shouting—"

I ran at him, slapping. He gripped the piñata under one arm, and held me off with the other, like I was a stupid kid, a puppet.

I pulled away from him.

He held the donkey like a boulder. "I don't want this."

"Touché."

I walked down the hall, my head high. His door clicked closed, quiet as a stab. It took all my strength to not look back, see if he'd abandoned the donkey in the corridor.

Back on the street, the night wind came at me again, whipped at my clothes the way Eddie used to undress me. From further down the street, kids' laughter sounded. We were going to get married someday, have two kids. How can that kind of love come to nothing?

The rain pelted. Sky the color of oil. Road choked with

vehicles. Sidewalk crawling with people. *Hurry, hurry.* The wind charged again, nipped at my cheeks and earlobes. At my car, I bowed my head against the elements and struggled to get my key into the lock. The city bustled about me, not missing a beat.

Fee Fi Fo Fum

Rose's caregivers insisted on removing her dentures before she napped, afraid she might choke now that she was shrinking and her teeth had gotten loose in her head. Rose refused to part with her dentures. The caregivers worked them out of her mouth.

When Rose awoke, she missed her teeth immediately, and pawed at her fallen-in mouth. The caregivers admitted her dentures couldn't be found. Rose bucked and shouted, and they pinned her shoulders, held her arms.

They laughed. "What's the panic? Were you going on a date?"

At dinner, Fat Greta, more blowfish than woman, tried to force-feed Rose watery gruel. Rose demanded they find her dentures. She wanted the roast chicken with trimmings, just like everyone else.

"You want to choke, is it?" Fat Greta rammed the spoon against Rose's lips and threatened to put her to bed if she didn't behave.

Rose snapped at Fat Greta's hand, sank her gums in. Fat Greta roared. Three caregivers swooped down and separated Rose's mouth from Fat Greta's rubbery paw. Rose reared backwards, crying out in triumph.

...

Rose waited for night, and then stole her way to the main bathroom. She felt her way in the dark, her slippers shuffling along the shiny linoleum. Inside the bathroom, she eased open the wall cabinet, unnerved by its groan. She listened for the night nurse's footfall. Nothing. She breathed again, and scanned the lines of drinking glasses inside the cabinet. Each glass contained a pair of dentures, its pink water flecked with food particles.

She reached a shaky hand inside the cabinet, and moved the glasses about. The glass labeled with her name remained empty. She froze, afraid she'd heard some movement in the corridor. The moments stretched. Her heart thumped dangerously. Sure she hadn't been detected, she resumed her search.

Toward the back of the cabinet, she found dentures inside a dry, chalky glass, the faded name on the label unknown to her. The dull ink read "deceased." Rose carried the glass to the sink and washed the dentures. They cleaned-up well, aside from the nicotine stains. Rose looked at her bony face in the mirror, her mouth deep in her head.

She inserted the dentures, and tasted mint and baking soda and tobacco. She fought the rush of nausea. Recovered, she bared the dentures and tapped them together. They fit well enough. Her smile wasn't hers, but it would do.

Back in the warmth of her bed, Rose pictured Fat Greta's face the following morning, when her new teeth found the caregiver's flesh.

Next to the Gutter

He arrived home from school and slipped into the dead feeling. As usual, the hallway was littered with purple Post-Its, so old they'd lost their stickiness. The first of his mother's notes read "EAT," followed by others with inked arrowheads that pointed to the kitchen.

On the fridge, a new note read "Milk's off, only good for tea." On the stove, the usual note in red marker, "Don't touch." He sat at the kitchen table, and lined-up crackers and the jar of peanut-butter. He moved aside the note on the napkin holder that read "After snack, homework."

In the living room, the yellow Post-It on the TV screen read "Don't you dare." In his bedroom, on his desk, she'd written on a ruled-sheet of yellow paper, "Check your homework <u>twice</u>." On his DS, "Only if you've done everything else." In the bathroom, on the toilet lid, her faded scribbles, "Flush. Wash Hands." Stuck to the front of the soap dish, "Count to ~~25~~ 50. Slowly!"

On her bedroom door, "Stay Out." His father had walked-out on his mother when she was pregnant, hadn't even waited to see what she'd give him. Lately, she'd taken to calling the boy the *man of the house*. Under his bedcovers, pinned to his flattened Paddington Bear, another new note, "Toss."

He returned to his mother's bedroom door, sniffed at its cracks and inhaled the traces of her face powder and spicy perfume. At six o'clock, when he heard her car pull into the driveway, he reached for the stack of orange Post-Its.

He waited inside the front door, Paddington Bear clutched to his stomach. His mother stopped short. He had stuck the Post-It to his forehead, "Free–Please Take." He pushed out past her, and took-up his position on the street.

The Big Top

I spotted the poster in the supermarket window, a large glossy sheet with a bright splash of words and colorful snapshots of the clowns, trapeze artists, and the Big Top. That evening over dinner, I suggested to my husband we'd go.

He sprinkled too much parmesan over his spaghetti. "What would bring us to the circus?"

"What wouldn't?"

He let the obvious hang in the silence.

We'd never managed to have children.

Over the next several days, I sulked, and tossed Jake only the odd word. I also went on strike about the house and refused to cook, to clean-up.

That night, as we prepared for bed, he asked, "This is over the circus?"

"Over your lack of interest in life, in fun."

"The circus? That's your idea of fun?"

The words almost choked me. "Yes, it is."

He removed his shirt, and used it to slap the bed. "Fine."

The night of the circus arrived. I wasn't so sure I wanted to go anymore. We'd likely be the only adults without children in tow. Also, to prove his point, Jake would refuse to enjoy himself. He was stubborn like that. Yet I couldn't back out, wouldn't give him the satisfaction.

We weaved our way around the excited kids and their frazzled parents, and shuffled through the sawdust and the strands of hay to our seats. Jake went in search of sodas and mustard pretzels. I could just about shut out the noise and revelry, the beaming children. I imagined that Jake and I were in a bar together, about to get silly and sexy like we used to. Afterwards, at home, we'd make love again like it was last thing we'd ever get to do. Trumpets blared and the stocky ringmaster in black top hat and red tails appeared. Jake rejoined me, pushed the cold soda cup into my hand.

Throughout the evening, I tried not to dwell on the children's delighted shouts and squeals, or on the animals, especially not the defeated elephants and big cats. The blue monkey was a sensation. He performed trick after trick, with cards, coins, and the ringmaster's top hat. He juggled six basketballs, and then five baseball bats. He was also fluent in sign language. Yet for all his brilliance, his dead eyes and eerie screech turned me cold.

On the drive home, Jake broke the silence. "They must have dyed that monkey blue?"

"I guess."

The silence returned. Jake turned-up the volume on the car radio.

The next morning, I walked downstairs to the kitchen, still in my pajamas and bare feet. The hardwood floors felt cold and were powdered in parts with the sawdust that had traveled home on our shoes.

Jake padded into the kitchen, his cow's lick high and yet to be tamed by gel.

Over coffee he said, "I can't stop thinking about that blue monkey."

My heart tightened. "Me too."

"Freaky," he said.

"Oh," I said.

I wasn't thinking freaky. I was thinking what if we could have brought the blue monkey home, rekindled his spark? If we held him. Loved him. Made him our own.

Crazy

In high school, Mrs. Hazel tried to teach us how to be good homemakers, how to earn our husbands' keep. She wore her red hair in a limp ponytail that hung almost to her buttocks, and had a sharp nose and chin, a witch's hazel eyes. After the first day of class, my friend, Marisha, said witch hazel was a skin tonic and had nothing to do with eye color. I insisted that witch's eyes were the hazel of a tree on fire, just like my mother's.

Mrs. Hazel joked that she married her husband for his name, and loved everything hazel, especially hazelnuts. She added hazelnuts to almost every dish, even omelets. We giggled. She rapped her knitting needles against her desk.

Home Economics proved to be my worst subject. My breads didn't rise, embroidery didn't make pictures, and knit socks with holes didn't pair. I didn't have the patience for so much repetition and exactness, for instructions and patterns. And why bother? I didn't ever want to be a wife or mother.

From the start, Marisha was Mrs. Hazel's star pupil.

"Why can't you be more like Marisha?" Mrs. Hazel asked. "You'd do well to follow her lead."

I quaked with temper. She sounded just like my mother, forever comparing me to my cousins and to my oldest brother.

...

The day I wore a black eye to class Mrs. Hazel asked me to step out into the corridor. She demanded to know how I'd managed to give myself something "so nasty." I pinched the inside of my left wrist and twisted the skin. The previous night, I'd rolled over in my sleep and hit my face against the window ledge. Earlier in the day, my sisters and I had moved our beds around, trying to make more space in our box bedroom. I felt tempted to lie, to tell Mrs. Hazel the black eye came courtesy of my mother, or my brother, both scenarios well within the realm of possibility. I told her the truth. Regardless, she didn't seem to believe me. I held her dubious gaze.

She ordered me back to class. "And no more collisions with window ledges, okay, Olive?"

My name always sounded so much worse out of her mouth, as green and slimy as the fruit.

Marisha wanted to get married just as soon as she finished high school, wanted to start a family right away and to have five children. I reminded her that it was nineteen-eighty-three, not the Dark Ages.

Marisha stuck up her nose, a nose not unlike Mrs. Hazel's, and said, "I wish you'd stop all this."

She about-turned, and marched off to the other side of the schoolyard.

I decided Mrs. Hazel was mentally ill. She wasn't crazy-crazy like my mother. She didn't see or hear things that weren't there or think that everyone was trying to kill her. But crazy comes in lots of different sizes and forms. Mrs. Hazel was the "too caught-up with domesticity" kind of crazy.

Every class, we suffered through a "show and tell" of her constant industry—the baby clothes she knitted for her friends' and neighbors' offspring, the dresses, tops, and pants she sewed for their older children. She paraded in front of us the fruit pies she baked and fancy dinners she cooked. She showed us hundreds of handkerchiefs, each embroidered with flowers of her own design. The way she held these items, and talked about them, touched them to her face, they seemed real to her, like children.

One afternoon, as Marisha and I rode the bus downtown, we spotted Mrs. Hazel standing outside Shaws department store. She was smoking, and repeatedly looked up and down the street, her thin neck stretched. She looked impatient and much too skinny, like the wind could pick her up and carry her off.

"I wonder who she's waiting on?" Marisha asked.

"Who cares."

Marisha fell back against her seat. "I want to be just like her when I'm older."

"Why?"

Marisha looked at me like I'd spoken Chinese. "She's amazing, that's why."

I looked out my graffitied window. "Amazing" repeated in my head like my mother's slaps.

"She smokes," I said, making it sound like a capital crime.

The dreaded day arrived. Mrs. Hazel had ranted for weeks about this class. We were to model our gingham aprons, cut from our very own patterns and painstakingly pieced together. Most everyone's apron was pink and white or navy and white squares. Only Marisha's apron had red and white squares, with five yellow heart daisies embroidered across its breast.

My apron sat gray and white and awful. Its hemline was too thick and the stitches were crooked. The neck strap was twisted and the pleats of the skirt were too bunched, its tie strings different lengths. I'd sweated into and toiled over the fabric so much its white squares had dirtied and wouldn't wash back to their original brightness.

I didn't want to model my stupid apron in front of the class. I'd have stayed home sick to get out of it only my mother was just back from another stay at the mental hospital, emptied now, a ghost. When Mrs. Hazel called on me to go up to the front of the class, I refused.

"It isn't optional, Olive. It's a class requirement."

Again, she made those pained faces, like my name was a mouth ulcer, like I hurt her eyes.

I was the last student she'd called on. My classmates all wore their perfect aprons, all turned in their seats to look at me. Marisha opened her eyes wide, communicated "get up there."

I dragged myself to the blackboard and faced the class. I pulled the apron over my head and tied it behind my back. I looked at the white space on the opposite wall, my face on fire.

Mrs. Hazel looked me up and down. "You just don't care, do you, Olive?"

I thought to run out of the classroom. Then, I knew just what to do.

I stroked the skirt of my apron again and again, a smooth dog, and made my voice as dead as my mother's. "You don't like my apron, Mrs. Hazel? I think it's pretty. Very, very pretty."

"Sit down, Olive."

I held up the apron's skirt by its corners and stared into its hollow. "Look, Mrs. Hazel, See, Mrs. Hazel. Pretty, Mrs. Hazel. So very pretty."

"I said to sit down, Olive."

I hugged the skirt to my chest. "Pretty, pretty."

"That's enough, Olive."

My smile remained fixed, my eyes unfocused. "Pretty."

I recognized the horror in Mrs. Hazel's face, the fear. It was there in my classmates too, in Marisha. The same terror I saw every day at home in the mirror.

Cut Through the Bone

Joyce greeted her eleven o'clock, Matt, in the spa's reception area and struggled to maintain her composure. He looked so much like her son, Tom. Tall, dark, and broad, in jeans and a sky-blue shirt, his face glowed, handsome in that "Jesuit college kid" way. She escorted him to the massage room, her legs rubbery and skin clammy.

She allowed him time to undress, and returned to the room.

He raised his head from the face rest and looked at her over his freckled shoulder. "I probably should have said right off about my leg?"

"You have an injury?"

"A stump."

She almost laughed but caught herself. Her eyes jumped to the flat space on the blankets where his right leg should have been, and to the prosthetic leaning against the wall. His embarrassment, and the nervous way he pushed back his hair from his forehead, again channeled Tom.

"Should I avoid the area?" she asked.

He resettled his head on the face rest. "No, go for it. Unless it makes you uncomfortable?"

"Not at all," she lied.

"It happened a couple of years ago. I took a tumble off my

motorcycle on the highway, met with a big rig."

She forced her mouth to work. "I'm sorry."

"Happens, it could have taken all of me."

Yes.

She worked Matt's lower back over and over, stalling.

He knew. "It's not that bad, honest."

She steeled herself, and lifted the sheet. His leg had been amputated several inches above the knee, its lumpy ends still an angry red and the three nubs like maggots in meat. Her stomach heaved.

She recovered her voice. "Let me know if the pressure's okay?"

"Just work it like any other leg, I'm good."

As she worked, everything in the small, dim space took on a haunted feel—the music and candles, and gardenia and sandalwood scents. The last time she had touched Tom, held him for any length, was at his high school graduation ceremony.

She worked on what remained of Matt's thigh, her pressure strong, deep.

Minutes later, he spoke again. "I know this sounds weird, but could you also massage where my leg used to be? It's the phantom stuff, I can still feel it."

She stared at the empty space, her heart knocking against her ribcage, and reminded herself to breathe.

"If you'd prefer not, that's cool."

She worked the air tentatively. He sighed long and deep.

"Can you get my toes?"

She placed her hands next to his left foot. "Here?"

"Perfect," he said, his voice thick with gratitude.

Warmth radiated out of her hands and into the memory of his foot, his leg, and all that was lost.

Acknowledgements

My deep thanks to the tireless editors who first published many of these stories, and to Kevin Murphy, large-hearted and dedicated, for making this book possible.

I am also indebted to Kevin O'Cuinn, for helping me get many of these stories where they needed to be.

To Victor LaValle, for helping and inspiring me more than he'll ever know.

To Matt Bell, Roxane Gay, Michael Kimball, Kyle Minor, Lori Ostlund, Meg Pokrass, William Walsh, Laura Van Den Berg, and Kevin Wilson, for their support and generosity. I remain honored and humbled.

To Jenn Coen and Jen Drew, for invaluable feedback.

To the bright memory of Amanda Davis, writer, teacher, light.

The Author

Raised in Ireland, Ethel Rohan now lives in San Francisco. Her work has appeared in *Guernica, Potomac Review,* and *Los Angeles Review,* among many others. Another short short story collection, *Hard to Say,* is forthcoming from *PANK* in 2011.

LaVergne, TN USA
11 January 2011
211910LV00001B/2/P